Katrina Ramos Atienza

WELL PLAYED

Patrice Reyes is starting her junior year at the University and she's convinced it's going to be the best semester ever. For starters, it looks like this is the year her team will win the regional football (soccer, for you Yanks) championships. Her subjects are looking good, and there's even a chance she might finally get somewhere with her rock star crush. But a new classmate—arrogant, cold Math nerd ('nuff said)—is seriously throwing off her groove. Will she ever get rid of him and have the awesome semester she deserves? Or is there truth to never judging (Math) books by their cover?

This book is dedicated to the UPLB Com Arts Society, who made my University experience complete.

Chapter 1

Up and down, like pistons; up and down, a machine, an engine; blood pumping through the muscles; skin warm despite the early morning chill.

Patrice Reyes, college junior and women's football varsity midfielder, had a brain fart: she pictured red blood, cool and silvery as it ran up her veins and fueled her muscles, much like gasoline, cool and silvery thing in high-tech car commercials.

She reached the top of the hill where the Infirmary was. Slightly out of breath from running on an incline, she paused and stretched. The morning was cool and still. Dew spangled the foliage that threatened to eat up the asphalt from the sidelines. It took a moment for her to remember that she was actually at the foot of the mighty Mt. Makiling, one of the Philippine's legendary summits, and the dense roadside greenery was its forests, always creeping towards the campus below and threatening to take back the civilized world into its jungle-y embrace. It was a lucky, lucky thing that she passed the exams to get into the University, she always thought; all summer long she missed the space and the silence and the wildness of the mountain, always just a ten-minute walk away, and a far cry from the crowded, cheek-by-jowl apartment complex she called home during vacation breaks in the city.

It was now ten minutes to six a.m., so she walked down the hill at an easy pace. It was going to be a good semester, she could feel it in her bones. She would ace all her academics and she would kill it in football. The whole team would, she vowed.

The memory of last year's semi-finals defeat still stung her: fighting tooth and nail against St. Clement's for eighty minutes had drained them all of their strength, but they still pressed on to break the 1-1 deadlock. Then came the St. Clement's captain, Marissa Cruz, a mountain of a woman charging down the field and parting the University's defenders like a hot knife through butter. A high ball sailed past them—too high, Patrice thought, to be a viable pass; but then Marissa leaped and, unbelievably, her head collided with the ball at just the right moment for it to change its trajectory and sink into the deep left corner of the net, seemingly miles away from the opposite space where their keeper had expected it.

But this year was *their* year. They were the best women's team the University had seen since the 1980s, everyone said so. It was all a matter of fulfilling their potential.

With these thoughts filling Patrice's head, she walked back to the dorm, almost oblivious to anything else.

It was the first day of the first semester at the University, and the smell of fresh *pan de sal* and sizzling *tocino* wafted out of Raymundo Street, a street teeming with apartments, dormitories, boarding houses, computer shops and cheap eateries that began at a chicken wire gate right alongside University land.

At the end of the street she caught sight of Alta Women's Dormitory, her home for the past three years. It was old yet well-kept; a 70s-era, two-storey wood-and-adobe house converted to meet the demands of a growing college town. Two middle-aged women owned it: a widow and her spinster sister.

Beside the old dorm was the newer, massive University Students Apartment, two monstrous three-story wings facing each other above the central unpaved parking lot and general party area. "U.S.A." was an unsupervised wonderland where the nights rang out with the sound of drinking and the apartments housed the gatherings of most of the University's fraternities, sororities and organizations. That previous night, U.S.A.'s parking lot hosted the traditional Welcome party, which marked the official start of class, and the housebound residents of Alta were forced to cower in bed with pillows against their ears to block out the noise.

Patrice ducked inside the kitchen door just in time to hear Mrs. Timbol, one of the dorm's owners, say: "Well, it's true. How is she supposed to attract a nice man if she's running around with raccoon eyes and a rat's nest of hair?" over the clatter and scrape of breakfasting college girls.

Aleli Carpo, one of the two punk rock band girls who lived in the room under the mezzanine, high-fived her as she headed out to class.

"She at it again?" muttered Patrice.

2

Aleli only rolled her eyeliner-smeared eyes as she trudged away.

Inside, Mrs. Timbol said, "You know—"

"College is the best time to meet your husband," Patrice finished for her as she burst inside. "We know." She grabbed a plate, piled it high with bread, meat, and eggs, and attacked the food ravenously, edging her roommate and best friend Gia Delgado from a bench as she did so.

"But that's what my mom said, too," said Deenie Lopez. Deenie was Patrice's *other* roommate, the daughter of Gia Delgado's mom's friend. From what Gia had told her, the new freshman with the upturned nose and blunt bob had several cousins studying at or were alumni of the University, two of whom were members of the Phi Gamma Chi sorority. Unfortunately for her, none of her cousins would make room for her at their apartments, nor would her mom allow her such unrestricted freedom as a freshman, so it was Room B with Gia and Patrice at Alta in the meantime.

"Welcome to the new millennium," Patrice said, her face stuffed full of food. "Last I heard we go to college to learn, not meet a husband."

"*Korek,*" said Miss Alya, Mrs. Timbol's sister, handing her a cup of coffee.

"Oh, don't listen to *Alya,*" said Mrs. Timbol. "She didn't pay attention to the boys then. Look at her now."

Miss Alya pulled a frown and then winked. She had heard this speech before, too.

"I met Mr. Timbol in Math class," said Mrs. Timbol, swooning slightly. Deenie and Isay, one of the other new freshmen, turned to her eagerly, while the rest of the girls tuned out to concentrate on breakfast. "He was such a looker. Always had perfectly pressed pants and these beautiful, starched white shirts...he'd pop the collar and roll up the sleeves, said it was too hot, but I knew he was a bad boy then, *tee-hee-hee*! We'd talk in class, yes, but one afternoon he asked me if I wanted to get a Royal with him from the Co-Op, and that was the start of a beautiful relationship." She dabbed at her eyes for effect. "I miss him every day, God rest his soul."

"How did he—?" asked Isay.

"Accident, dear, very traumatic. A truck swerved into his lane. Died instantly."

"Oh. Sorry."

"I am too, dear." Mrs. Timbol deflated slightly. "But that is not the point. The point is I would not have met Mr. Timbol had I wandered around campus looking like a refugee. Or like a sweaty tomboy," she pointedly glanced at Patrice, "all dark from the sun and eating like a construction worker."

"I'm with the varsity!" she cried. "I've been running since five a.m. and I need to refuel, you know!"

"Five a.m.?" asked Miss Alya, now washing dishes.

"I'm trying not to over-train," said Patrice. "Plus there's more practice this afternoon."

Mrs. Timbol made a *tsch* sound. "Well, *she'd* be sympathetic because she remembers her varsity days with you, dear. A lot of good *that* did for her love life."

"I wouldn't be able to study here if I weren't with the varsity," Patrice muttered.

It was sometimes incredible to remember that Mrs. Timbol and Miss Alya were actually sisters. In appearance as with personality, the two were most unlike. Miss Alya was tall and wiry from a lifetime's obsession with athletics, and she still began her day, as she did for the past thirty years, at sunrise with a brisk walk around the Oval. Rain or shine. She had a plain, lined face and spoke sparingly. Mrs. Timbol, the younger one, was as round and soft and bedecked as a throw pillow, tactlessly rambled like she knew best for everyone else, and always played matchmaker with her tenants. Turning away from Patrice, she zeroed in on Gia and began her favorite pastime.

"Gia, dear, have I told you about the boys I ran into at U.S.A. yesterday? Very handsome fellows." Her pudgy fingers wrapped around a cup of coffee. "I sold them one of our spare mattresses."

"Here we go," said Miss Alya. "Mrs. T. will not rest until all of you are engaged."

"I failed with you, Alya, I do not want others to suffer the same way."

"Yes," said her sister. "Such a pity. All those years *not* washing another man's socks…" The girls stifled a giggle.

4

"Laugh all you want," said Mrs. Timbol, turning into the color of a clay pot. "Mark my words, girls. When you end up old and alone and unloved one day, you'll wish you'd listened to Mrs. Timbol over at Alta!" She huffed out the kitchen, banging the screen door with a clang as she dramatically swiped her hair and clutched her chest. Patrice chortled, irritating Mrs. Timbol all the more, so she took her vengeance on a poor green parakeet imprisoned in the dorm's patio.

"The heartlessness, Koko! Look! All I do, and what is my thanks? Teased and laughed at…"

Gia's pretty face frowned. "Patrice, I wish you wouldn't tease her that way," she said. "I better go check on her."

"You're a saint, G," said Patrice. "I don't deserve you for a roommate." She gulped down the last of her meal and dashed upstairs to get ready for class.

Deenie followed Patrice and Gia down Raymundo Street to the University's chicken wire gate. Gia was instructing Deenie on what to expect from the University: where her classes were located and where to get on and off the jeepneys, paying no mind to the male stares that lingered on her over the stream of students walking to and from the University.

Patrice, too, received her fair share of looks, but instead of ignoring them, as Gia did, she was actually completely oblivious. To be fair, her thoughts were full of anticipation for football practice that afternoon—she had practiced over the summer, when she could make the trip to the University, but this would be the first time the full squad would be complete, and she wanted to see if their positions would be changed or if the newly promoted first team sophomores would make a big difference in their game.

"You two are popular," remarked Deenie. "All the boys are looking at you."

Patrice frowned, looking down on her plain denim shorts, hiking sandals and FC Barcelona jersey, as if expecting to suddenly see a fashionable outfit.

"Well…" said Gia, smiling politely, "Um…We better get to class." She hailed a jeepney, threw Patrice a confused look, and ushered Deenie in. Patrice waved them off as she crossed the road to the grassy lawn in front of the College of Management, following her favorite shaded path to the Humanities building. The ground was a bit wet from the early morning dew, and her sandals soon trailed mud, but nothing recharged her more than a quick walk and some sun.

After a couple of twisty turns the Humanities building soon loomed before her. She loved this old building, with its red steps worn smooth by decades of hanging out students, two stubby wings on either side of an open central area with the College Secretary's offices and a free-for-all bulletin board. The building also housed three *tambayan*—broad wooden tables with built-in benches on either side, kind of like a picnic table, but a bit more meaningful to the University. Every officially recognized organization in the University got one, and it was unofficially recognized that non-members could never ever sit there unless by invitation of the org's members—a fact that a hapless freshman was now realizing as the members of the Sociology Society gave him dirty looks for parking his butt on their bench. On the opposite wing, on the way to her classroom, was the *tambayan* of the Organization of Literature, Speech and Dramatics Majors (or, as it was known simply throughout campus, The Org), populated by many of Patrice's classmates. She waved them quick hellos, nodded at other familiar faces, then ducked inside her classroom.

As she caught up with old acquaintances, she noticed a man seated at the far end of the room, beside the windows, watching the rest of them with a steady gaze.

A tiny girl, clad in equally tiny shorts, caught her eye as she entered and glanced at the mysterious brooder. Bit-Bit Velez was the president of The Org and knew anyone who was anyone at the University .

"Who's that?" Patrice whispered.

Bit-Bit tossed her head, pretending to adjust the straps of her top. "Darling, I have no idea," she whispered back.

"That's impossible!" Patrice breathed.

"Well, I think —I'm not super sure—that I've seen him with the Phi Delta Phi guys. But not often, so I don't think he's one of their *brods*. He's cute, though."

"If you don't mind being frowned at all day."

Bit-Bit was laughing loudly, that a special brand of high-pitched cackles that irritated so many professors, when their young instructor walked into the classroom. Patrice hurriedly scrambled off the armrest of Bit-Bit's chair and joined the rest of the students stampeding for the best seats in the room. In the rush she was jostled farther and farther away from the door, and found herself seated beside Mr. Frowny Brooding Dude.

The young professor introduced herself as Nadia Alunan and asked them for their class cards. Patrice pulled hers, added it to the pile being passed to the center of the room and extended her hand to the man beside her, but instead of handing her his card as in polite student etiquette, he stood and passed the card directly to the instructor's hands. The instructor, who had been telling them to call her Ma'am Nadia, watched him as he took his seat.

"Mr. Paul Dalmacio," she said, reading the card. "An Applied Math major! Guys, we have a rare specimen in our midst. What brings you to the Humanities building?"

The attention, instead of bringing a grin from the man's face, turned his expression sterner.

There were a few awkward moments before he spoke: "We're required a Humanities elective."

"I know that, Mr. Dalmacio, but usually your types go for the reading and analysis courses. But this is Expository Writing. Papers every week, and no short ones too."

He sniffed irritably. "I solve complex math equations daily. I'm sure I can manage...*papers* every week." He almost spat out the last three words.

Patrice rolled her eyes, and Bit-Bit's eyebrow arched. The Bachelor of Arts kids were used to being condescended to by the students taking up BS (Bachelor of Science) courses—saying that Communication Arts was a soft course, one that anyone could take, especially those who had failed in Engineering or Physics and would do anything to escape dismissal from the University. But to face that condescension in *their* territory, the Humanities building, and in their class too, was incredibly insulting. Patrice's mobile phone silently vibrated in her pocket. As the instructor recovered her composure and went on with her introduction, she peeked at a text from Bit-Bit.

"I will have my *brods* beat him up," it said.

Considering that Bit-Bit was the president of The Org and that her *brods* were mostly gay theater majors, the text solicited a loud, surprised guffaw from Patrice. Ma'am Nadia glanced at her as she quickly stowed the phone away.

"Yes, Miss…?"

"Reyes, ma'am. Patrice Reyes. Sorry, I have, uh…allergies."

Bit-Bit's shoulders convulsed with laughter as Patrice bit her cheek from smiling again. She could feel her seatmate's eyes on her face. She threw him an exasperated glance—a Medusa stare that usually forced the most boneheaded of fratmen to turn away—but this man, this Paul character, only met her glance with a steady, challenging look. She purposely turned her back on him and tried to concentrate on every word Nadia Alunan was saying.

The instructor, perhaps for the benefit of the overconfident Applied Math major, now enumerated every paper they were to pass that semester. Patrice had just caught the words "…a fifteen-page prose piece or narrative essay to be composed with your seatmate" when she cried: "Ma'am! Which seatmate?"

Nadia looked at her like she had two heads. "The one on your right of course, Ms. Reyes."

Patrice took advantage of the sudden din of talking students to face Paul, who only deigned to glance back. She leaned toward him.

"Pao, is it?"

"It's *Paul*."

"Right." She tried to smile sweetly. "Looks like sooner or later we'll have to work together on this fifteen-pager."

He smirked, almost imperceptibly, but did not answer.

Patrice then resolved to ignore him forever and ever and possibly find a new seat, and a partner, for the next class. Surely there would be newcomers who didn't bother attending the first day of class, and among those stragglers she would be sure to find a partner who wasn't Paul the Applied Math guy. Having made up her mind, she put all her irritation away and concentrated on the class and the lecture, which, taking the arrogant seatmate out of the picture, was actually quite interesting.

The class was soon dismissed, and Patrice laughed and talked as she went to her next one. She was so busy catching up and greeting friends that she did not notice the lingering stare that Paul Dalmacio, Applied Math major, gave her as he crossed the road to the Math building.

Chapter 2

One afternoon a week later, Patrice sat slowly stirring a cup of coffee in Alta's kitchen, her face was still warm and swollen from a long midday *siesta*. Gia sat across making notes on legal pad. Patrice was just about to take a bite from the heap of Spanish bread on her plate when the kitchen door clanged and Deenie burst in, red-faced with excitement.

"Oh my God you guys!" squealed Deenie. "I just found out that—" and here she paused for dramatic effect "—the Freshman Shindig is happening this Friday!"

"So?" Patrice said. "It happens every year."

"*So?* I'm dying to go!"

"Then go," said Patrice. "Freshmen get in for free."

"I know that," Deenie answered irritably. "It's just that—"

"What's going on?" said Mrs. Timbol, emerging from the mezzanine and looking peeved that her afternoon *teleserye* was being disturbed.

"It's the Freshman Shindig this Thursday!" said Deenie, who finally found an animated confidante in Mrs. Timbol. "I'm so excited to go!"

"Oh, dear, that's exciting! Phi Delta Phi sponsors it, and they always have the handsomest boys. What are you wearing?"

"I don't know yet, Mrs. T—I'm not sure I can go." Deenie pouted, her voice falling.

"Why not?" said Mrs. Timbol, taking her by the shoulder.

"Mom doesn't want me partying by myself," she said. "Especially at a frat-sponsored event. She's worried I'll turn out like one of my cousins. She…she said she'll only let me go if Gia calls her up and tells her she's going too."

Gia looked up. "Me?"

"Please, please, please Gia, I'm so dying to go, please?" said Deenie.

"I don't know…" said Gia.

"You're wasting time, Deenie," said Patrice. "She didn't even go when *she* was a freshman, and everyone was saying she was a sure to be Ms. Freshman Shindig. The girl falls asleep at nine, hello!"

"Yes, Deenie, it's really not my thing..."

"Then just tell mom you're going! Just call her up and...and you wouldn't have to go..."

"I couldn't do that!" said Gia. "Your mom specifically asked me to look after you and—"

"So please, go with me!"

"Come on, Gia, give the poor dear a chance," said Mrs. Timbol. "It's not every year that you can go to the Shindig and be the star of the party." A crafty expression stole over her face. "Tell you what. Why don't you take *all* the freshmen to the shindig? There are those two dears at Room A, I'm sure they'd love to go."

Gia smiled nervously. She looked at Patrice for help, but Patrice only shook her head and mouthed *No*. Mrs. Timbol was now crouched on Gia's right, stroking her hand and pleading along with Deenie.

"Please please please, Gia—"

"Now, dear, don't you want your roommate to have fun?"

"Giiiiiaaaaa! Please please *please*?!"

"Oh...okay," Gia sighed. "I guess I could go."

The kitchen was drowned with the squeals and screams of Deenie, who immediately ran upstairs to tell the girls in Room A about their good fortune. Mrs. Timbol patted Gia's head like a prized poodle then returned to her soap opera.

"You *have* to go with me," Gia turned suddenly to Patrice.

"No way."

"Patrice. *Patits*." Deploying Patrice's childhood nickname meant she was all business. "Please?"

"Look, Gia, I told you to say no."

Gia only clasped her hand and stared with round, pleading eyes.

"I hate those stupid things!" cried Patrice, pulling her hand free. "All those fratmen and sorority girls milling around like they owned the place, eyeing the freshmen like cuts of meat—"

Gia face fell. "It's okay, Patrice." She rallied with a brave smile. "Really, it's fine."

Patrice groaned into her coffee. "All right. All right! I'll go."

"Thank you, thank you!"

"How much are the tickets to that again?" Patrice grumbled.

On the night of the party Patrice huddled on an ottoman in the mezzanine, half-concentrating on the game show on TV and waiting for the freshmen to get ready. Pam Ong (Aleli's mezzanine roommate/bandmate) and the seniors in Room C were busily shouting the answers to the hapless contestant on the show. Patrice managed to chuckle a few times at the woman's stupidity, but on the whole she was very annoyed at having to spend a Thursday night at something as useless as a fraternity *dance*.

A door upstairs closed and down the stairs came Isay with her roommate, Rebecca Jobilo. Rebecca seldom came out of her room, and when she did, she was always accompanied by a thick *manga* comic book. She read these in Japanese, which, she explained to Isay, she had taught herself in order to enjoy her favorite anime without the subtitles. One night she left the dorm completely costumed as a samurai. Mercifully, tonight, Rebecca was normally dressed in a straight-cut cream dress that fell to her knees, her coarse hair held back by a wide polka-dot headband.

Isay nervously smoothed her own skirt and blouse. "Am I...overdressed?" she asked, noticing that Patrice only wore a trim yellow shirt, dark jeans and her only clean shoes, a pair of cream canvas ballet flats that she hated wearing.

"Well hey! You're sort-of dressed up," remarked Pam, turning from the TV set to appraise Patrice. "I mean, for *your* standards."

"Speak for yourself!" laughed Patrice, throwing a cushion at Pam.

"What, this?" she tugged at her laddered gray t-shirt and ran her fingers through her harsh buzz-cut hair. "My uniform, man."

"You're fine," said Patrice to Isay. "As Pam said, this is as dressed-up as I get."

Heavy shoes clomped down the wooden steps, announcing the arrival of Deenie. She sashayed in a tiny black skirt, a halter top, black tights and high wedge sandals. The seniors hastily closed their gaping mouths at the sight of her. Gia, looking positively dowdy in contrast in a blue sleeveless top and jeans, followed nervously behind, trying to throw a shawl over Deenie's bare back.

Mrs. Timbol materialized from the kitchen, clasping her hands in delight. "Deenie! You look like a model! Gia, dear, maybe you'd like to wear a skirt too?"

Gia shook her head. "Oh, I don't think so, Mrs. T. I wouldn't be comfortable."

Mrs. Timbol then produced a tube of lipstick from her pocket and pounced on Patrice, who instantly began cowering. "Just—a—tiny—dab, dear —" she said, trying madly to catch Patrice as she wriggled away. "You look so pale, and I do wish you'd do something different other than that tired ponytail!"

Patrice dashed out the kitchen door, grabbing Rebecca and Isay by the hand. "See ya, Mrs. Timbol! Let's go girls!"

Gia, who finally managing to drape the shawl on Deenie, followed. As they walked down the road to the jeepneys, she fell in step with Patrice, behind the freshmen who were excitedly speculating about all the cute boys they hoped to see at the dance.

"You owe me," said Patrice.

"I know, Patrice, I'm real sorry," said Gia.

"Well, at least I didn't have to pay for my ticket."

"I'm really, really thankful you came. You know how I hate staying out late like this."

"I know." Patrice ushered the girls into a jeepney packed with other dressed-up freshmen. "Let's just make the most out of it, all right?"

The jeepney stopped in front of the Hall of Human Kinetics: a large, rectangular building with crumbling pillars out front. It was dominated by an airy, high-ceilinged basketball court where the campus parties were held. Thumping hip-hop music swelled from the entrance as the jeepney passengers got off. Isay gaped at the knots of students laughing and flirting by the parked cars and at the line of sophisticated sorority girls manning the ticket tables. Deenie took everyone's tickets and walked confidently to one of them.

"Hi!" she chirped, smiling widely. "I'm Deenie."

The tickets were taken by a girl with a prominent chin. With not a strand of silky hair out of place, she could have been pretty save for an expression of perma-disdain on her face. She spared a bored glance at Deenie before nodding them in. Deenie, however, stayed put.

"You're Marga Mañalac. We met last sem," she said.

Marga raised an eyebrow. "Aren't you a freshman?"

"Oh, do I look older?" she replied excitedly.

"With all that face paint…" drawled Marga, and two of her sorority sisters giggled.

"Deenie," said Patrice, "I don't want to spend the entire night out here." Deenie, however, remained behind, and they could still make out her chatter of "I'm Pia Lopez's cousin…yes, yes, at the party at her apartment…you were only there for a while but I remember…yes…"

"Gia, you better get her before Marga sics the dogs," said Patrice.

"Who was that?" asked Isay.

"Like Deenie said. Marga Mañalac, president of Phi Gamma Chi, the sister sorority of Phi Delta Phi."

"Is she…mean?"

"Only if you let her." Patrice spied Bit-Bit in the middle of the dancing crowd. "Girls, you go and have fun. I'll be back in a bit."

Bit-Bit saw Patrice coming from across the hall and let out a loud cackle. "Patriiiiiiiiiiice!!" she cried, stumbling forward with a cup of punch, air-kissing people as she went. "Of all the people to be here!"

"I was taken hostage by the freshmen," said Patrice.

"Freaky little creatures, aren't they?" said Claude, one of Bit-Bit's org brods. Most people were scared of Claude: he wasn't very tall, but he had a stocky build and, coupled with his ever-present paper fan, perfectly groomed eyebrows and scowl, an imposing aura. He was now grandly watching the crowd. "Every year. They get smaller and uglier."

"Oh Claude, don't be such a bitch," said Bit-Bit. "Ooh, wait, there's Bing! I have to say hi." Dragging Claude by the hand, she ran to the opposite end of the court.

Left to her own devices, Patrice found herself a plastic cup of the free spiked punch and a pillar to lean on. A couple classmates saw her, and she was soon coaxed to dance. Then her cup emptied, the slight buzz from the punch kicked in, and her naturally active self overcame her initial awkwardness.

She joined a group of people dancing in a circle with their high-heeled shoes heaped in the center like a bizarre bonfire. The group grew larger and then broke into smaller circles, and Patrice now giggled happily with Isay and her blockmates. The music segued easily, building until the speakers trembled and they all felt the bass reverberating in their bones, making them dance with abandon. Taken by the music, Patrice and the freshmen raised their hands in the air like they were on a rollercoaster, cried "Whee!" in unison and then jumped up and down on invisible pogo sticks. Suddenly Patrice found herself being twirled around in a silly bastardized swing by Claude, who had likewise forgotten to bully the freshmen. She closed her eyes in a swirl of disco lights and booming music and laughed happily.

"Girl, sweat check!" cried Bit-Bit, who had materialized by her elbow. "You've been dancing non-stop!"

Patrice laughed again. "Man, that punch is strong."

"Nah, admit it, you were having fun!"

"Yeah, I guess I was!"

"Might I persuade you two in a party circuit?" said Bit-Bit. "Just in case you'd like to rest and, you know, mock people."

"Delicious idea!" said Claude, and the two of them linked their arms into Patrice's to drag her away.

Their progress around the hall was halted every now and then by greetings with Bit-Bit's extended network of friends. Patrice's ears were filled with the music and the non-stop commentary of her companions:

"I didn't know she was a nocturnal beauty!"

"What do you mean?"

"She looks great...in the dark!"

"Oh God, *he* got fat."

"I used to find him so hot when we were freshmen."

"That girl's shoes are so tragic."

"Forget the shoes, girl, her make-up is trademark *Funeraria Paz*!"

"Mmm-hmm, girl. If you can't afford a salon don't go to a mortician!"

"That freshie over there's acting like it's Spring Break in Florida or something."

"Ugh, *please*."

Patrice jerked her head and saw Deenie grinding with another scantily clad girl, sandwiched between heaving, bobbing guys, her shawl nowhere to be seen. Gia stood off in a nearby corner, sway-stepping with two friends, but still keeping a nervous eye on Deenie.

Then Patrice noticed a handsome man standing a few feet from Gia, watching her intently like he had never seen anything quite so intriguing. Patrice had run into him from time to time near the Engineering building during her jogs. She recognized his easy smile, smooth, tanned skin and hair that looked like he spent hours getting it at the just the right level of "effortlessly messy." He looked friendly and easygoing—quite unlike many other fratmen who swaggered about with scowls on their faces, like they were perpetually looking for a rumble.

Every now and then he answered some question from his companion, a nervous, ferrety-looking guy who scanned the hall repeatedly. Otherwise, he seemed oblivious to anything else but Gia. Patrice was just about to ask who he was when Bit-Bit bent her ear.

"Migs Fuertes looks like he's crushing on your roommate there."

"Mm-hmm!" said Claude, snapping his fingers.

They stopped to watch. The ferrety-looking fellow suddenly left, leaving Migs to approach. He greeted the girls dancing with Gia warmly, and one of them stopped long enough to introduce them to each other. Migs and Gia shook hands. He leaned in to say something that made her laugh. Gia's two friends inched away, which she didn't seem to notice. Patrice watched Gia talk and laugh easily with Migs, and noticed how his eyes were never off her friend the entire time they spoke.

"Normally I'd claw her eyes out," observed Claude. "But I have to hand it to Migs, he could not have replaced me with a better-looking girl."

"Dream on, Claude!" said Bit-Bit. "Come on, let's circulate some more!"

They passed by Rebecca with a group of cosplayers— kids in elaborate, anime-inspired costumes—while Rebecca lovingly inspected the fake swords, kimonos and wigs worn by her friends, looking like she would die of envy.

Claude nudged Bit-Bit and they snickered at Marga, who was obviously trying to shake off the ferrety-looking guy who had been with Migs earlier. She weaved and bobbed in the crowd, cutting him off as he followed her.

Every now and then in their circuit they would come across Deenie talking, dancing or laughing, each time with a different guy.

At the end of one lap they parted ways: Bit-Bit to dance, Claude to powder his nose, and Patrice to Gia and Migs, whom she spotted at the edge of the room, near the shadow of the exits. She hesitated to approach, seeing them so engrossed with each other, but Gia had seen her and waved excitedly.

But then the face of Paul Dalmacio, Applied Math major, stern as ever, came into the meager light.

With Gia gesturing to her and Migs and Paul watching, she could not turn away. Forcing a smile to hide her dislike, she joined them.

"As I was saying, Migs, this is my roommate and closest friend, Patrice."

"So nice to finally meet you," he greeted her warmly. "I'm a big fan."

"Whuzza—?"

"I saw you at a couple of meets last sem. You're an excellent midfielder! Fastest I ever saw."

Patrice did not expect this compliment and blushed deeply.

"Excuse me, this is my friend, Paul—"

"We've already met," said Paul curtly. Patrice was too charmed by Migs to be annoyed.

"I hope you're enjoying yourself," Migs said. "Gia says you don't often go out."

"Yeah, we usually stay in," said Patrice. "I'm normally worn out from football and Gia's always studying."

"I'm afraid Patrice is making me look like a big nerd!" laughed Gia, a little self conscious.

"Well, I'm glad you made the time," he said to Gia. Turning to Patrice, he added, "Paul here pointed you out earlier. You dance pretty well."

"Um..." said Patrice, embarrassed as she remembered how she jumped and hooted on the dance floor. "You were watching that, huh? I must've looked like a fool—"

She glanced at Paul, who stared steadily back. He probably expected Migs to make fun of her, except his friend was less of a jerk than he wanted.

"He, on the other hand, can't dance if you bribed him!" Migs added as Paul winced. "I told him maybe he should ask you to dance so he could understand how much fun it really is—"

"Not on your life," muttered Paul. Patrice caught the remark.

"How sad," she said, in exaggerated tones of pity. "You never dance?"

"No."

"Never? Not alone? In your room? When a cool song comes on the radio? Never?"

Paul looked uncomfortable. "Well—I—"

"How sad." Patrice repeated. "But I guess you're a lot more fun with a complex equation in front of you, eh? Nothing like algebraic expressions for some excitement in your life, right?"

Migs laughed, unaware of his friend's embarrassment.

Marga suddenly reappeared, having shaken off Migs' ferrety friend. "Paul!" she trilled, not-so-gently pushing Patrice out of the way. "Have you just arrived?"

"He's been here the entire night," said Migs. "Hiding out in the shadows and watching everybody dance and have fun."

Marga's expression was sympathetic. "Oh I know *exactly* how you feel, Paul. These things do get tiring, don't they?"

"Really? You didn't seem to think so when we were freshmen," said Paul.

"Oh—well—that was two years ago, you know how we outgrow that phase!" she said. Paul did not seem to want to continue talking and turned towards the dance floor.

"Migs!" said Marga, as though she had not been rebuffed. "Who are your friends?"

Patrice could've gagged on her plastic display of friendliness as Migs introduced them. She could barely muster a smile in her direction, although Marga and Gia instantly fell into conversation on some shared professors.

Her present company's desirability dwindling by the second, she spied Isay and her friends in the crowd, and better still, she heard the opening beats to her favorite song. Calling out "Excuse me!" to Migs and company, she ran to them and was welcomed back eager yells of excitement.

The song began. Screaming the lyrics at the top of their lungs, their eyes shut in the moment, Patrice and the group danced and jumped wildly. By the first chorus, Claude, Bit-Bit and their friends in The Org joined the circle, and by the second, Migs and Gia were dancing in the center. Patrice laughed happily as she watched them shyly glancing at each other as they moved, Gia always poised and graceful no matter how excitable everyone else got and Migs gamely trying to catch her hands.

Patrice was also aware of Paul and Marga still standing in the corner, watching them. Whenever she happened to glance their way, she saw Marga intently and continuously whispering in his ear, no doubt judging them all, while Paul stood with that maddeningly grave expression on his face. The more she talked and he stared, the more Patrice intended to horrify them by dancing all the wilder. Soon they were following Claude's lead, who instructed them in a complex choreographed jazz routine, and not much longer after that, they all raised their hands above their heads like they were on a rollercoaster, cried "Whee!" in unison and then jumped up and down on invisible pogo sticks.

"That should give them loads to talk about all night," thought Patrice, noting Marga's scandalized expression. "Those two deserve each other."

Chapter 3

For two weeks after the Freshman Shindig, talk in the dormitory was dominated by no other subject. Deenie endlessly recounted how she had been voted Ms. Freshman, starting with how she and three other "finalists" were approached by Phi Delta Phi members, how, at 11pm, they were called on to the raised stage where the DJ spun to dance before the crowd; how she out-danced everyone and flirted with the DJ; and, finally, how the crowd was asked to applaud for their favorite and that she got the loudest cheers. After the fourth or fifth edition of the story, which became more and more detailed with each retelling, Miss Alya broke her usual reserve and banned the mention of the Freshman Shindig in her presence. Patrice made it a point to sit near Miss Alya at dinnertime after that.

Gia, Patrice noticed, was suddenly frequently invited by Marga to Phi Gamma Chi activities, from sorority-sponsored contests to after-dinner get-togethers at U.S.A. At first, Gia said that she only went to accompany Deenie, who never turned an invitation down and was angling on being recruited. Unfortunately, Deenie's mother—and the College Secretary eventually—banned freshmen from joining any organizations.

With Deenie forbidden to join and the chance of recruiting Gia very slim (she was a junior, after all, and would never allow herself to undergo the initiation process), Patrice often wondered what purpose Marga had in mind for the constant invitations. Curious, she accompanied Gia to one picnic, held after the sorority's annual charity book drive, and realized the true reason for it all: Migs was always present, and his attentions to her friend were obvious.

Unfortunately, where Migs went, there too was his friend Paul, and Patrice found him so irritating that she declined any further Phi Delta Phi or Phi Gamma Chi invitations. It was bad enough to spend an hour and a half of class twice a week with him, his condescending remarks, and his unsettling stares. She wanted her leisure time to be as Paul-free as possible.

Besides, with the football varsity's first major game coming up, Patrice's leisure time was very limited indeed.

Three afternoons out of every week were spent in grueling practices, and the remaining afternoons as well as all her mornings were spent running and lifting weights, at her coach's insistence to build up stamina.

Thursday's practice was particularly brutal. A sudden hard rain interrupted their session, and when they returned to the field, the sky had darkened and the ground was soft and mushy.

"Excellent!" cried their coach. "This'll teach you to take any conditions you get. Remember, girls, we've never played the new field at St. Clement's before, and I want you to be prepared."

"Whatever you say, coach," said Patrice.

"Is it really the time for that 'whatever, coach' attitude?!" scoffed the coach. "We can never be over-prepared for St. Clement's," he continued maniacally. "They demolished us last year and I don't want to lose to them again."

"But coach!" wailed Kitty, the team captain. "We can't even see the ball, it's so dark!"

"Then you'll learn to *sense* it," said the coach.

"The guy thinks we're ninjas," muttered Catch, one of the defenders, as they lined up for the drill.

"OK, guys, big mixed bag!" cried the coach as his assistant rounded up the team in groups of five. The coach stopped in front of Patrice's group. "Kitty, Janina, pair up; Patrice, Catch and April, defend. I want to see crisp passing and defending! If you get the ball, take it to the goal. Defenders, I want you on your toes—do not let anything in, girls. Right. Go!"

With a blast from his whistle the players were off, running and scrambling on the field. Kitty and Janina, the attackers, viciously drove forward while Patrice and the defenders did their best to protect the ball and confuse the opposition. The wet soil made the ball easier to control but threw off their running altogether. After a scoreless half, the coach switched their positions, and Patrice was now urged to score a goal. Kitty and Janina blocked her at every turn. Flicking the ball upward with her toe, she passed it with a high volley to Catch, who speedily dispatched it to the goal posts with a powerful (and muddy) header. Anette, the keeper, tasted earth in her scramble to block the ball, though it still crossed the line with a squelching *thweulrp*.

"Excellent teamwork, guys!" cried the coach. "Good hustle, Anette. Er, you have mud on your teeth."

"Coach," groaned Patrice. "We can't see a damned thing. This is more mud-wrestling than football. It's dark and we're cold and hungry. Could we please, please, please stop?!"

The coach raised his watch to his face and started. "Er, yes, it's almost eight…"

"What?" yelled Catch. "I have a paper to do…gotta run!" Without waiting for the coach to wrap up his pep talk, she gathered her gym bag and ran to an idling jeepney in front of Human Kinetics.

Patrice sat dazed with exhaustion, stretching her legs out and guzzling water as the coach peppered them with tips. His pep talk, their long walk from the field to the Student Union building and then the business of eating their meals—consumed in an exhausted and sullen silence—ate up so much of what Patrice longed to be sleeping time.

When the squad finally broke apart, her longed-for rest was delayed once more with a text message from Deenie: "Come quick. Gia sick @ U.S.A."

Patrice arrived at the apartment complex in a panic, brusquely asking the first familiar-looking Phi Delta Phi member where her roommate was. Apparently, H-5, Migs Fuertes' apartment. She dashed up the steps and ran the length of the second-floor hallway, mumbling apologies to the singing, drinking and talking students hanging out in her way. At the end of the hall she found Deenie silhouetted against the rails with two other guys.

"Where's Gia?" she asked breathlessly.

Deenie giggled. "Inside."

Patrice studied her glassy eyes and flushed cheeks. "Did you get her drunk?"

"No-o-o," she sang. "All her fault. Tee-hee! Told her the chocolate milk wasn't what she thought."

Patrice rushed inside. Like the rest of U.S.A. apartments, it was a narrow space with two bedrooms to the right and a kitchen and bathroom at the end. There was a long bench and table near the door. Empty beer and gin bottles were arranged like a shrine under the kitchen sink. A beat-up egg-yolk yellow fridge hummed in a corner. Migs stood uneasily outside the bathroom door, sweating buckets. The ferrety-looking fellow she had seen at the Freshman Shindig stood from the bench and offered his hand.

"Jon Lee," he said. Patrice was surprised to hear such a deep voice coming from such a thin guy. "Phi Delta Phi president."

She clasped his hand and gave him her special Medusa stare. "What did you do to my roommate?"

Jon stammered something about Marga and the sisses going to H-5 to join them for drinks, but the more he spoke the more livid Patrice's expression became.

"Where is she now?" she demanded.

"Patrice, I'm so sorry," Migs said, hurrying to her side. "Marga and the sisses brought gin and chocolate milk...gin-o-colate, they call it...they asked Gia to try some. It was half a glass, I swear, I didn't know she would react so badly."

"That's because she doesn't drink!" exclaimed Patrice. "And that's the sickest concoction I've ever heard."

Patrice wrenched the door open to find Marga—her normally sleek hair plastered to her face with sweat, her bare feet drenched with water—hunched behind the kneeling Gia, who was slumped over the toilet.

Patrice knelt. "Gia? Gia?! Come on, girl!" she shook her friend.

Gia's eyes fluttered, struggling to focus. "Pat...rice...," she whispered. "I'm...sleepy."

"Don't worry, she's puked everything in her stomach, she won't mess up the sheets," said Marga, voice on edge.

"That's nice to know," hissed Patrice, lifting Gia's arm as Marga took the other. They pulled her up and out the bathroom. Gia could stand, but just barely, so Migs relieved Marga of the weight.

"Sorry," Gia told him.

"No, *I'm* sorry," said Migs. "I shouldn't have let you drink. It was stupid of me."

Gia smiled slightly. But then her head dropped forward and her eyes closed. Migs jerked in alarm, which woke her up. "I...I just have to sleep," Gia said.

Migs led her to his room, the one closest the front door. Patrice shouldered it open and was greeted by two hopelessly rumpled mattresses on the floor, heaped with clothes and beddings and towels and pillows and readings. A wire rack overflowing with used clothes; and gadgets, books and papers moldered in the room's corners. Clearing the debris with his knee, Migs and Patrice let Gia down his mattress. She immediately curled up and slept soundly.

"I'm sorry for the mess," said Migs as they closed the door behind them, noticing Patrice's horrified expression. "I share the room with Jon...we, uh, don't get to clean very often—"

"How long do you think she'll be out like that?" snapped Patrice.

"Two to three hours, hopefully," said Jon confidently from the bench.

"Look, Patrice, we can take care of her, we'll take her home once she—" Migs began.

"Absolutely not!" said Patrice. "If you think I will leave her here, after you practically *poisoned* her…!"

"Don't overreact," Marga said. "It's not a big deal!"

Patrice was on the verge of saying something very insulting when suddenly the second bedroom door opened and out came Paul Dalmacio, looking very annoyed.

"And what are you doing here?" Patrice yelled.

"I happen to live here," he answered coldly.

Patrice blushed with embarrassment. "I thought…you weren't Phi Delta Phi," she managed.

"I'm not," replied Paul. He lingered at the doorway as Migs quickly explained that Paul, while not a fraternity brother, was his close friend and shared the apartment with them. The explanation ended in silence. Jon was nervously fidgeting in his seat and Patrice, Migs and Paul all remained frozen to their spots. Marga was trying to smooth her hair and wipe away her sweat at the same time.

"We, could, um, all have a seat, you know," suggested Jon. As Migs took a plastic stool by his door, Patrice sat beside Jon and, with the ache in her calves and thighs more pronounced after the initial surge of anger wore away, unconsciously stretched her legs.

Marga wrinkled her nose at the sight of her muddy socks and cleats, but Paul, who had removed a stool from his

24

own room and positioned himself beside Migs, quietly watched her flex her limbs.

"Sorry," said Patrice, catching his eyes. "I'm afraid I've muddied up your *mansion*."

Jon coughed. "How'd you get so…?"

"Football practice," Paul answered at once. "From the rain, I bet."

"Clever," said Patrice. "Must be that logical, mathematical brain at work."

"Not at all. Just common sense," said Paul.

Marga laughed, realized she was the only one, and stopped.

Migs began apologizing again. "Patrice, please believe me when I say how truly sorry I am for all of this. I take full responsibility for all that happened. I didn't make her drink the stuff, that's true, but it's my place and I should have kept a closer watch on her."

"You talk like she's five years old!" Marga suddenly exploded. "The girl's twenty, for God's sake, I'm sure she can take care of herself. If she got drunk it's her own damned fault." Eyeing Paul triumphantly, she added: "Personally, *I* never cared for girls who can't hold their liquor. I'd never go to a party without making sure I can leave it standing up."

The door crashed open and Deenie stumbled in. "Thatssh true, Marga," she slurred. "We girls can go home by ourselvesh." Then she fell into Jon's lap.

"I…uh, I think I'll take her back to the dorm," he muttered.

"Wait! Wait!" said Deenie, lifting her head. "I have shometing to shhay. There'sh shometing wrong…"

"Go home, Deenie," said Marga, cradling her forehead.

"N-no! I have to…to shay shometing…"

"What about, Deenie?" asked Jon patiently.

"About Gia…drinking…isshh not her fault…She said she didn't want any… Marga…Marga shaid ishh only milk…jusht a drop of gin…makeshit tashte like Bailey'sh…but I shaw you pour half the bottle in!"

Jon propped her up on his shoulder and stumbled a little.

"It was just half a glass!" Marga protested. Migs, Patrice and Jon stared at her. She tried to appeal to Paul, the only

25

person whose expression remained blank. "If I knew she would react so badly, believe me, I wouldn't have given her a shot of the stuff. I mean, God, how many people do you meet in the University who can't drink loads of this stuff? Huh?"

Even Jon looked disappointed at her.

"Well!" she said, standing up with as much dignity as she could muster. "If she's going to cause this much trouble over gin-o-colate, I'm *never* inviting her again." She fumbled for her shoes and, with her nose in the air, pushed past Jon and Deenie.

"Um...guys...I'll be back," said Jon, hoisting Deenie up and dragging her with him as he followed Marga down the hall.

"Hey! You bring Deenie home!" Migs called.

He re-entered and sat beside Patrice, who had shut her eyes and bent her head back in exhaustion.

"Patrice..."

"Yes, *I know*, you're sorry," she sighed, rubbing her aching neck. "I don't doubt you mean it. I'm sorry I yelled at you too. I'm just...so...tired..." and here she stifled a huge yawn.

"I can make you coffee while you wait for Gia to wake up," said Migs.

"That would be perfect. Thank you."

While Migs boiled water and hunted for a clean mug, Patrice leaned as far back as the bench allowed, resting the back of her neck against the backrest and stretching her legs out again.

"I hope you don't mind me stretching out like this," she said to Paul, her eyes still closed—and therefore unaware of how uneasy he had become at the sight of her long neck exposed before him, her skin still flushed from football practice and her legs stretched out so close to him. He cleared his throat to mumble "No."

"I'm soooooooooooo tired," she said again.

"The sooner the season is over, the better, then?" asked Migs.

"I wish it were done," said Patrice. "No—wait, I shouldn't wish that all! Football is the only reason why I'm even here."

"Football—as in soccer," Paul said.

"Paul, you philistine, only Americans call football 'soccer'!" said Migs.

Paul ignored him. "So you're on varsity scholarship?" he asked Patrice. His tone was calm and even, but Patrice thought she could make out the disdain in it.

"Yes, I'm on scholarship," she answered. "Not only do I have to play hard and play well, my grades have to be good too. Double pressure. But that's a small exchange for free tuition, plus a little room-and-board allowance." Paul stared at her. "I doubt you'd have any idea what I'm talking about," she said.

"You're a fantastic player, Patrice, and Gia tells me you do really well at academics," said Migs.

"I don't know a lot of varsity players," said Paul. "Most of them seem to be in the BA courses."

Patrice arched an eyebrow. Was that *another* veiled dig at her course? "So what are you saying? That BS students are sickly nerds who can't play sports?"

Migs laughed loudly. "You've just described half the Applied Math guys I know. Excluding you, of course, Paul."

"Oh really?" said Patrice, straightening in her seat. "What's your sport? Chess?"

"Basketball," muttered Paul.

"Basketball's a dumb game," said Patrice dismissively. "Classic example of mass delusion. It's funny how Pinoys think they can actually be good at the sport when most of us are too short to play it anyway."

She didn't actually feel that way. She had tremendous respect for the hardworking basketball varsity team, who were often overshadowed by high-profile squads from other schools, but she wanted to belittle Paul in whatever way she could, since *he* seemed to put her down all the time.

"But football, now that's something Pinoys could be good at, if it were only more popular," said Migs, handing her the mug of coffee.

"Precisely," said Patrice. "Height is not that important in football. You just need speed, agility, stamina. I bet you it's only a matter of time until we qualify for the World Cup."

At this remark Migs and Patrice began talking animatedly about their favorite World Cup moments, which Premiere League teams they were rooting for, their favorite players, what prospects the Azkals had of ever making the World Cup, and other football arcana.

Paul felt more and more out of place at the conversation. In a lull between the excited stories of Migs and the technical explanations of Patrice, he said:

"Migs tried to get me to watch a match on TV once. British teams, I think."

Patrice nodded but did not dignify the remark with an answer, and she and Migs excluded him again from the conversation.

"I read this blog once," he said, loudly. "The reason why riots break out during football matches is because of boredom." Heedless of Patrice's shocked expression and Migs' pointed glance, he continued: "Two teams take an hour and a half to score what, one or two goals? Sometimes none at all? The fans get violent just for something to happen."

Migs lowered his face into his hands.

"Spoken like a true basketball fan," said Patrice coldly. She smiled as she said this, for it confirmed all her suspicions about Paul: he was a man who was so inflexible and so arrogant that he belittled her major and insulted her beloved sport. It was clear he had no redeeming qualities whatsoever.

If she was honest with herself she had to admit there were times when she wondered if she had been too hard on him. That maybe the bad first impression he made might've been a misunderstanding, or a product of truly awkward social skills. But *now* she knew without a doubt that she was free to vehemently dislike Paul Dalmacio, without any guilt at all.

The conversation continued on to other, more general subjects—the amount of rain in the University, the lack of jeepneys, the smell of mold in the Main Library—while Paul remained resolutely silent, yet refused to go back to his room. After an hour Migs checked on Gia and found her awake and well enough to get home. Patrice helped her up and, together with Migs, walked back to Alta, away from the scene of Gia's mounting embarrassment—and away from football-bashing Paul.

Chapter 4

The first half of the semester quickly passed and before they knew it, the girls of Alta found themselves huddled in their chosen corners, all furiously studying for the mid-terms. The mezzanine was taken over by the three seniors of Room C, who littered it with notes and photocopied papers, their laptops scattered every which way so that no one could watch TV. The freshmen were almost always in the kitchen, where they would often be cornered by Mrs. Timbol and her tips for getting good grades. Patrice and Gia retreated to the relatively peaceful patio, where the breeze passing through Mrs. Timbol's wind chimes and the chirping of the parakeet relaxed them.

Unfortunately, Pam and Aleli, for whom mid-terms were only a minor nuisance, loved the patio as well—for band practice. Patrice and Gia were studying one stifling-hot Tuesday when a blue pick-up pulled up, the rear crammed with musical equipment. They watched curiously as Pam and Aleli bounded out and began unloading guitars, amps and drums and stacking them in the patio.

"Are you—?" asked Patrice.

"Sorry, girls, practice today," said Aleli briskly.

"It's two in the afternoon!" said Patrice. "Everyone's asleep."

"Miss Alya gave us the go signal," said Pam, uncoiling a length of cord, setting up the amps and plugging in the guitars. Gia looked on helplessly as Pam and Aleli's drummer, Lars, appeared, carrying a bass drum. Patrice momentarily lost interest in her notebook as she watched him expertly assemble the drum kit.

"Patrice," he greeted, noticing her.

"Hey," she replied. She untied her ponytail and smoothed down her hair.

He took his seat behind the kit and lightly drummed, adjusting the positions of the cymbals. It was some time before Patrice realized she had been openly staring at him. He caught her looking and flashed a sweet grin.

Patrice blushed. Lars Capili often had that effect on the girls at the University. He had a confident, unassuming air about him, and watching him play the drums—his cherubic lips pressed together, boyish face frowning in concentration—was an occasion for mass swooning. Thoroughly rattled, Patrice began gathering her things together and mumbled to Gia that she would continue studying in the library. She couldn't help it. No matter how long she had been acquainted with Lars, and no matter how familiar she was with his bandmates, she still couldn't help being a tiny bit affected by her crush on him.

"Going so soon?" he called as she stood to leave.

"Sorry…I, uh, have to study for an exam," she stammered.

"That's too bad," he grinned. "I thought you were gonna listen to us."

Patrice could only swallow her reply, though Gia remained composed. "Maybe next time, Lars," she said politely. "Patrice, I'll be upstairs."

Aleli and Pam tuned their instruments and Lars still grinned at Patrice.

"Um, I gotta—" she began.

"Hey, are you watching our end-of-exams gig at U.S.A.?" he asked.

"When's that? Can't on Friday. Have to be up early for a Saturday game—"

"No, not this Friday. Next Thursday." He smiled hopefully. "Nine days from now. Will you be there?"

"Sure, sure," she said hastily.

"Promise? I want to see you, OK?" he said.

"Promise," said Patrice, turning so that he wouldn't see the bright red flush of her cheeks or the equally bright smile on her face.

At the library, Patrice managed to plow through a few pages of work before the memory of Lars saying he wanted to see her at the gig kept interrupting her thoughts. She kept on replaying the scene in her head: him sitting behind the drums, sticks poised over the cymbals, the sun coming in through the garden and bathing his face in golden light so that he looked more rock star-handsome than usual. What got her about Lars was that unlike the other (very) few conventionally cute guys in campus, his good looks were balanced by an air of manly scruffiness: his head was shaved, he had a bristly goatee and he dressed very casually, almost carelessly, in old graphic T-shirts, faded jeans and dirty sneakers. Lars didn't believe in hair products or accessories or presentable clothes, and this appealed to her very much.

After an hour of struggling with her notes, she decided to give up and go for a run so she could exercise (and, it had to be said, fantasize about Lars uninterrupted). She left her notes with the guard on duty and crouched to retie the laces on her sneakers. It was at this point—bent over on the steps of the library, her hair hanging down her face—that a familiar voice greeted her.

"Afternoon, Patrice."

She looked up. Her face fell at the sight of Paul Dalmacio.

"Hmph," she said, by way of greeting. She straightened, wanting very much to be on her way, but he blocked her and seemed in no hurry to move. He opened his mouth to speak, attempting several sentences and rejected each one.

Finally, he decided on the question, "Studying?"

"Just finished, actually," she said. "I'm going for a run."

"Ah," he said.

Several moments passed without a word being said.

"I have to—" Patrice began.

"So, you like to run?" he asked at the same time.

She stifled a groan. "Yes. It's a core skill for football, you know." He nodded, did not add another word. She decided that this would be the best time to outline her territory to Paul to prevent any further encounters with him. "I often go along the back of the library. On the Never-ending Bridge, you know. Then up the hill to the Infirmary, for conditioning. Then I do some laps around the Oval."

"Ah," he said again.

"Well—goodbye!" she cried, dashing down the steps.

Two days after their encounter on the library steps, she saw a familiar silver Toyota park behind the library, and soon after met him at the foot of the Never-ending Bridge just as she started her jog. He hastily explained that he was on his way to study, but instead of leaving her alone and crossing to the building's back entrance, he followed her all the way to the end of the bridge, in total silence, and only turned back when she started up the hill to the Infirmary.

Patrice began to wonder if there was any truth about the rumors of dwarves, elementals and *nuno sa punso* lurking in the woods near the Infirmary, and if she had inadvertently stepped on one of them on her run, because bad luck seemed to dog her at every turn. That Friday, her team lost against St. Clement's. It was only for the group round and the squad could still make the quarter-final stage if they beat the two other schools in their bracket, but the pain of losing to their worst rivals—in addition to the aches of their bodies, because the St. Clement's girls played very physically—was deeply felt. Her coach yelled and screamed and was only appeased when Kitty informed them that she heard two key players from the opposing team of their next game were both injured.

"Excellent!" cried the coach, as though a sprained ankle and a pulled tendon were the best things to happen to a couple of girls. "Without the captain and their first keeper we'll beat them easily. We're a shoo-in for the quarters!"

The squad was about to breath a collective sigh of relief when the coach added, "But then we'll surely meet St. Clement's again in the next tournament stages! Guys, I'm increasing our practices. Be at the field one hour early next week, all right?"

If this wasn't torture enough, the following Monday morning, Patrice found Paul and his friend Migs running around the Oval as well. Her morning run, which she looked forward to as "me time," was interrupted by Migs jogging alongside her and constantly peppering her with questions about Gia.

Patrice tried to evade them as best as she could. Gia had been mortified by her experience at Migs apartment and had avoided him at all possible costs, going so far as to take another, longer route to the campus so that she wouldn't encounter him along Raymundo Street. Patrice knew that Gia only did that because she genuinely liked Migs, which magnified her embarrassment at getting drunk at his apartment. Patrice had explained several times that it was not her fault but Marga's, but Gia could not be swayed. Of course, she could not reveal any of this to Migs, so the best she could do was say, "She's, uh, really busy with acads."

That Monday was especially accursed, because at her Expository Writing class, the instructor paired her and Paul together officially for their fifteen-page prose piece or narrative essay. Patrice tried to explain her preference for another partner to the instructor without mentioning the words "hate him with every fiber of my being," but Nadia Alunan was firm.

Patrice wanted to cry. On top of the pressure from the mid-term exams and her increasingly insane football practices, she now had to find a way to work with Paul without giving into the urge to smack his head with a rolled-up handout.

She was so upset that she couldn't even manage an answer when Paul asked to meet her for dinner on Wednesday, after her practice, to discuss their paper. She nodded curtly, silently punched in her number into his phone, and raised her eyebrows in reply when he asked her if she was OK.

Her only consolation was that all this time, Pam and Aleli practiced constantly at Alta's patio, and where Pam and Aleli practiced, there was Lars. Their gig was coming up that Thursday, and all Patrice had to do was get over the unpleasantness of her dinner with Paul before finally being able to unwind at the party—and see Lars.

Chapter 5

On Wednesday night, Patrice dragged her tired, aching body, still clad in her drenched jersey and cleats, to the campus mall for the dinner meeting with Paul.

She brushed past the clumps of students withdrawing money from ATMs, smoking, scrounging for free Wi-Fi and hanging out to get to the second-floor restaurant where she was to meet Paul. The place was dim and cozy, with wood-paneled walls and booths. Wicker baskets hung on the ceiling along with trailing plants and brightly colored cushions dotted the seats. Paul was already seated in a booth, seriously contemplating his cell phone.

"Hello," she said breathlessly. She dumped her gym bag on the seat and threw herself on top of it, resisting the urge to rest her head on the table and just go for a long snooze.

"I was waiting to see if you'd text," said Paul.

Patrice's ears pricked up but she was too tired to be irritated. "I was only ten freaking minutes late, Paul," she said listlessly.

He watched her close her eyes and rub her temples for several seconds.

She felt his gaze. "Can I help you?"

He looked away, probably embarrassed she'd imagine someone like him staring at someone like *her*. "Do, you, um, want to order?" he handed her a menu.

"Fine, whatever."

As the water took their orders the air felt charged, curiously tense.

"So, boss, what's the plan?" she rested her chin on her hand.

He shuffled his notes. "I, uh, thought we could do a narrative essay."

"Hm," said Patrice. He stared at her again.

"A narrative essay....of what?" she said.

"I—I thought you might have an idea."

Normally this would be the perfect opportunity for her to let loose with some cutting remark at the unsuitability of his Applied Math skills and sarcastically bemoan her poor BA Communications qualifications, but she decided against it. She wanted to get this over with. Besides, if there was one thing she never played around with, it was her academics. If playing nice meant turning out a good paper that allowed her to maintain her grade point average—and her scholarship—she was prepared to endure the worst of Paul.

"Let's see," she began. "It's a two-person project, and this is Expository Writing, so obviously there's a lot of description and explanation required. We can't both do our own thing and splice it together. It has to be cohesive. So we have to decide on a shared topic and pull the paper together based on that. We could do a 'he said, she said' thing. You know, capitalize on our contrasts." The waiter arrived; she took a sip of water.

"Our contrasts," said Paul.

"Yes, Paul. Contrasts. Differences."

"You think we're very different from each other?"

"Hel-*lo*?" she raised an eyebrow.

"Like how?" he pressed.

Patrice looked around her. "Well—for one thing, this restaurant."

"What about it?"

"Do you come here often?"

"All the time. I know the owner."

"See, I've only been here twice in my three years at the University."

"Why's that?"

"Can't afford it," she said bluntly.

Paul blanched. "I wish you said something—"

"Don't worry, one overpriced meal this semester won't reduce me to poverty. And look, I wasn't trying to make you feel bad—I'm just trying to make a point."

His gaze seemed to search her face. "And that point is?"

"Is that we're completely different."

He remained silent, but his expression was incredulous.

"You're Mr. Analytical Applied Math who hardly speaks and doesn't dance and hates football and looks down on the arts students," she said hurriedly.

Paul's composure was unruffled. "And if I were to go by your argument, I would state the opposite: you are Ms. Illogical Communications major who blurts out whatever comes to mind, makes a fool of herself on the dance floor, would kill over a simple thing like football and resents the science students."

She swallowed a lump in her throat. "Fair enough," she said, struggling to contain her shock. "I never really doubted that was what you thought of me."

"But then you'd be wrong," said Paul quietly.

"But you just said—"

"What I said was modeled on *your* argument. I simply took your words and said the opposite, so as to illustrate my point."

"And your point is?" She leaned forward, challenging him.

"I don't think of you that way at all."

"Huh," scoffed Patrice. "And how *do* you think of me?"

Paul suddenly leaned back, seemingly irritated. The waiter arrived with their baked macaroni, but the tension on the table remained.

"I think of you very differently," he finally said, in a very soft, strange tone of voice that Patrice strained to hear.

Patrice did not know what to answer. He was now looking at her with a gaze that she could not read—it seemed to try to tell her something—but what, she did not know. Slightly flustered, she concentrated on the macaroni.

Silently he watched her eat. Then he cleared his throat and said, in a much more businesslike tone, "I understand your suggestion about capitalizing on, as you said, our…contrasts."

She nodded.

"What do you think about us each describing a specific event, so that they run parallel to each other? It would have to be the same event, of course," he added.

"That works," she said, in a way that she hoped sounded casual. "What event?"

"It could be a childhood memory. Or a shared situation."

"I doubt you have any situations to share with me," said Patrice.

Paul looked irritated again. "I think there are common experiences regardless of social status. First plane rides, first kisses, favorite toys, major parental disagreements—"

"I've never been on a plane—yet," she argued. "And I'm an orphan."

She bit her lip, silently scolding herself for blurting that out—to him, of all people! Miss Alya knew some of her story, but it was only Gia who knew it completely. Most of the time she had hoped to pass for having parents abroad.

He looked at her for a long time with his hard-to-read eyes.

"Don't pity me," she said finally, forcing calm into her voice. "My aunt has been taking care of me since…um, and Miss Alya is like a second mom. Money is tight, yeah, but then there's football and that takes care a bit of that. I'll graduate soon and earn myself, and anyway, it's not really a big deal."

"When did you lose—" said Paul uncertainly. "—when did they pass away?"

"My dad died when I was a baby," said Patrice. "Mom was always sickly. She, uh, lived with her sister, my aunt, obviously, and they both looked after me. Then in high school—well, that's when Mom finally followed Dad. I was, I don't know. Thirteen, I guess."

She picked at the macaroni, and for several minutes both of them ate in silence.

"I was four," said Paul quietly.

"Huh?"

"I was four when my parents, you know—" he explained.

Patrice did not know quite how to react. He hung his head low, like a child, and suddenly she longed to reach across the table and hold his hand. "I'm so sorry," she said.

"No," he said abruptly. "Don't be."

She debated if she should ask him how it happened, but he startled her by saying: "They were on a boat to Bacolod. We had some relatives there. My grandfather told me that Pa wanted to take the plane, but Mama was scared of flying. It, you know…the boat. It sank. Made the news and everything. I don't remember much, actually. My grandparents have clippings and stuff, but I don't want to look at them. I mean, obviously."

"Your grandparents raised you?" asked Patrice.

"Yes."

He blinked several times, sipped water, cleared his throat and had a few bites of macaroni.

"So," he said, and now he sounded distant once again, arrogant and direct. "Would you like to write about that?"

"Yes. I mean, well, if it's OK with you—"

"Yes, yes, that's fine," he said quickly.

"Oh," said Patrice. "Well. We could do around six pages each of our essay. That comes out to twelve pages."

"Obviously," said Paul. "I remember having to do fifteen pages, yes?"

This was said so rudely that Patrice's ears tingled. "I know that. I'm not deaf or stupid, I remember our instructions too. We'll do six each. That leaves a page for the intro and a couple at the end to tie the whole thing together."

"OK," said Paul, avoiding her gaze.

"So. Six pages each. Do you want to work together on doing the intro or will you trust me enough to do it myself?"

"But—"

"I'm might be a lowly arts student but writing's one of my main skills, even if you think it's laughably simple."

"I didn't say that!" he said.

Patrice took a deep breath to steady herself. Why was she so rattled by him? Why was she so annoyed at his change of tone? She held very still, composing herself. Finally, she managed a tight grimace.

"Right. Well, if you have no strong objections, I'll do the intro and the tying up. OK?"

Paul looked like he wanted to argue, but stopped at the steely glint in her eyes. "Fine."

"Great," she said, faking a smile. "Email me your stuff next week"—she texted him her email address—"and I'll work on it over the weekend. We'll polish it on Monday and pass it on the next class."

"Yes," he said, sounding strangely disappointed.

They finished their meal in silence, only speaking to argue over the bill. He wanted to pay for her meal, she felt insulted, and after a heated exchange, he agreed to go Dutch. She gathered her bag and stood to leave.

"How are you getting home?" said Paul.

"Walking," she sniffed.

"I have a car, I could just take you—"

"Well, shoot. I just forgot, I have to pass by the grocery downstairs, get some supplies," she said, making it up as she talked.

"It's almost ten. The grocery's already closed," he said stiffly.

"Well—I—"

"That's fine," said Paul. "Fine." He stood and gave her a brief, stiff, formal kind of nod, which seemed almost a bow. Patrice resisted the urge to curtsy. He looked at her for several moments, seemingly distressed, and she waited for him to say something, anything. But then he nodded again and quickly left.

Patrice lingered at a stack of magazines by the restaurant's waiting area. After ten minutes, and fully confident that she would not meet him on the streets, she finally left herself.

Chapter 6

Patrice burst into her dorm room late on Thursday afternoon to find Gia curled in bed, half-propped against the wall and staring out the window.

"Gia!" said Patrice, unloading her things, rifling through her drawers and collecting her toiletries. "Where's Deenie?"

"Somewhere," Gia said, tracing outlines on the window. After a few moments, she wrenched herself from the view of the dorm's laundry area and watched Patrice choose shirts. "Where are you going?" she asked.

"What do you mean? Aleli has that gig tonight at U.S.A."

"Oh," said Gia, staring out the window again.

"Well?" asked Patrice, her hands on her hips. "Aren't you coming?"

"I don't know," she said.

Patrice sank down beside her on the bed. "You're not going?"

Gia shrugged.

"Come on, it'll be fun!" said Patrice.

She sighed.

Patrice leaned on her friend. "What's wrong, G?"

She sighed again. "I—I kind of don't want to run into Migs."

"Gia!" Patrice began.

"I know, I know, it's not my fault, Marga's really mean, etcetera, but still. I'm *soooo* embarrassed about it. What must he think of me now? Throwing up in his bathroom, passing out in his bed…oh God, I don't even want to remember," she buried her face into the pillow.

"You know, he still asks about you," said Patrice, patting her hair. Gia was still hidden behind the pillow, but her shoulders tensed.

"Remember last week? When I was talking about running into Paul—again!—on my jog? Migs was there."

Gia's eyes appeared. "He was?"

"Oh yeah," said Patrice casually. "Pissed me off, you know, running beside me and asking 'Gia this' and 'Gia that', he really threw me off."

Half of Gia's face was now visible. "What did he, um, ask about me? What did you say?"

"G," said Patrice in all earnestness. "He likes you. He really, really does. I don't think he minds one bit that you got sick at his place. In fact, I think he enjoyed it."

Gia's eyes widened. "What do you mean?"

"I don't mean he's sadistic and weird and got off on you being helpless and stuff. I just mean that he must've felt real cool, you know, 'rescuing' you like that. In a good way."

Her whole face was now visible. "Really? You think so?"

"I *know* so," said Patrice.

Gia now smiled. "So you think—you think he'd be OK, with me talking to him now after ignoring him for the longest time?"

"Well, put it this way—if he won't be OK with it, then he's a jerk and not worth it."

Her face fell a little.

"Come on, G, I don't think that's how he's going to take it," Patrice chided. "Will you please, please come with me to the gig already?"

"Oh…" trailed Gia. "Oh, OK, I guess I could. I might as well unwind, yeah?"

"Yeah, right, you're really going there to *unwind*," teased Patrice.

"Ha!" laughed Gia. "And you don't have *other* motives for going, no?"

"Mid-terms have just finished! I've been in total stress these past few weeks. We have that game this weekend…I need this!" she cried at the increasingly wide smile on Gia's face. Then she smiled as well, thinking about Lars: Lars behind the drums…lips clamped in concentration….the sweat beading above his mouth…those sexy eyes glancing at her every now and then….Patrice was almost lost in her daydream when Gia called her back to earth.

"So Paul has nothing to with it," said Gia.

The vision of Lars crashed and burned. "*Paul*? What?"

"Oh…but I thought…"

"You thought what?"

"I thought—well, I *think*—he really likes you."

Patrice laughed harshly. "Are you nuts? Of course not! The man hates me. And—and *I* hate him too."

"Oh," Gia said again. "It's just that…oh, never mind."

"It's just that what?"

"Nothing," said Gia. At the funny look on Patrice's face, she continued: "Well, OK. It's the way he looks at you. I noticed it before, well, before I started avoiding Migs."

"Maybe you were drunk." It was a joke but came out blunter than she meant.

"Yeah, but still. He just has this look in his eye that—"

Patrice stood. "He's only looking for things to criticize."

"All right," Gia sighed, throwing up her hands in defeat. She got up and rifled through her clothes. "What are you going to wear?"

"Jeans. This shirt," said Patrice, holding out a red-and-white striped tank top.

Gia smiled. "So you're just there to unwind, but you're using your sexiest shirt?"

Patrice stuck out her tongue. "I just wanted to use this—!"

"Patits, tell me! Who's the guy?"

She hesitated before answering: "It's Lars."

The smile was still on Gia's face, but it had frozen into place.

"What's the matter?"

She quickly turned away and busied herself with the clothes. "Oh, nothing."

Patrice waited for a few moments. Eventually Gia stopped pretending to inspect a white puff-sleeved blouse to say, "There's just something about him that's…kind of…off."

"Off?"

Gia wet her lips, searching for the right words to say. "It's nothing in particular, really," she began. "He just has this way of talking that comes off as...hmm…*insinuating*, I guess. Like it's all very calculated."

"What!" laughed Patrice. "He's just polite."

"He's a bit of a flirt, if you ask me," said Gia softly.

Patrice was about to argue more when she remembered Lars' easy smile and all the swooning he induced in girls. She changed tactic. "Well, flirting's not so bad. Everyone flirts."

Gia shrugged. "Just—I don't know, just be on guard, right?"

Patrice smiled tightly. "Are you taking a shower or can I go first?"

As Patrice and Gia walked to U.S.A., they could hear the thrum of electric guitars and the deep boom of bass drums. In a few short steps they were engulfed by a crowd of people.

"It's like New Year's Eve!" laughed Patrice as Gia smiled nervously.

Inside U.S.A. more people crammed into the lot between the two apartment wings, many clutching clear plastic cups of beer. More people lined the railings of the wings, watching the action in the relative comfort of the small spaces in front of their apartments. Gia scanned for any familiar faces in the rails in front of H5, but the mass of people was too thick to see anything.

Patrice dragged her through the crush to get close to the stage. There were many familiar faces that, in the small community of the University, they didn't really know but still greeted with nods. Every now and then they stopped to chat with people they *did* know—Bit-Bit Velez and Claude with a group from The Org, Rebecca and two kids in ninja costumes—but they made their progress steady and determined. Feeling like they had been squeezed from a womb, drenched with the sweat of strangers and out of breath themselves, Patrice and Gia found themselves in front of the makeshift stage, draped with a banner of a skull on a bass drum above two crossed guitars and the words:

"UNDERGROUND MUSIC CLUB: MID-TERM MASSACRE"

A large, burly man with a scraggly moustache and lank, wavy hair was erupting in guttural howls in front of them, while two guitarists, a bassist and a drummer banged out the crunch-crunch-crunch rhythm of death metal. Gia winced and quickly pulled Patrice just as two skinny, shirtless men started moshing. Her timing was perfect, because the area they left turned into a mass of writhing, slamming, heaving bodies.

"I wonder when Aleli's coming on," said Patrice.

"WHAT?" yelled Gia, inching away from the blasts of sound shooting from a large speaker in front of them.

"ALELI!" yelled Patrice, pointing to her watch, then to the stage, and then shrugging.

"AH!" yelled Gia. She, too, shrugged.

The death metal band lurched into two more songs. Patrice thought she could make out Aleli and her band in the dark stairwell off the left wing, with a group of Underground Music Club members. Still scanning the rails, Gia turned and saw a group of Phi Gamma Chi girls hanging out in front of Marga Mañalac's first-floor apartment. One of them caught her eye, whispered to the girl next to her, and laughed.

Finally the death metal dudes finished, and the host climbed on stage to applause mixed with ironic booing and not-quite clever catcalls.

"Give it up for The Maggots!" yelled the host.

"Get down!"

"They rot!"

"They stink!"

"Boo!" yelled one of the formerly-moshing-but-now-heckling skinny guys.

"Our next band is a campus legend," continued the host, ignoring the hecklers. Behind him, Patrice saw, feeling like a balloon inflated in her belly, Lars getting up the stage to fiddle with the drum kit. Pam followed, plugging her bass guitar into an amp and playing a few notes, while Aleli tested her pedals.

"They've been playing together for five years, describing their sound as punk mashed with Kylie Minogue," said the host, reading off a piece of paper. The crowd hooted with laughter.

"They need no other introduction—"

"—So shut up!"

"—LEZZ BE HONEST!!!"

Aleli swaggered to the mic, her eyes dark moons of eyeliner-smeared smudge.

"You got balls?" she yelled.

The moshers grabbed their crotches and raised their fists into the air.

"I don't believe you!" she screeched.

"I'll show you!" screamed one guy.

"I'm Aleli and I'm going to rock your ballsacks off, you skinny losers!" At this her guitar roared to life and joined the pounding drums and the thumping bass in a crescendo of mad, driving punk rock.

The music surged through the crowd like the shockwaves of a bomb. A collective roar issued from the throng, and soon the whole apartment complex pogo'd up and down to Aleli's voice.

Patrice and Gia let themselves go to the music. It was as if a primal scream were released from the center of their beings, and giving into the yell freed some integral part of themselves that spent most of its time trapped and hidden. Gia regained some semblance of control after the initial scream, content with slight head banging, while Patrice tried not to fall over anyone as she leaped and danced with abandon. From time to time she would open her eyes to see Lars looking straight at her with an appreciative smile that made her weak in the knees.

The band launched into each song with energy and passion, like their lives depended on this one performance. Aleli was at the lip of the stage, pressed against the mic stand with one leg propped against a monitor, snarling as she sang. Pam, who was normally laid back, plucked at her bass with intense concentration, like a shaman trying to raise the dead with a song. Lars played furiously, and with each bang of the drum and clash of the cymbal the crowd felt their frustrations and aggressions systematically released.

At the flourish that marked the end of their set, Patrice leaned back, raised her hands to the air and let loose a yell of exhilaration. Lars winked at her. Flustered, she turned away to compose herself—only to see Paul, just a few people away in the crowd, watching her intently.

She faced the stage again and clapped appreciatively. As the band exited, she risked another glance and saw he now stood next to her. She decided to be civil and gracious.

"Isn't this great?" she smiled. "You must feel so lucky to have gigs like this at your building all the time."

"I'd much rather sleep," said Paul.

Patrice faltered mid-clap.

As she watched the new band set up on stage, Paul remained at her side. She could feel him there, standing still like some sort of weird statue and spreading Eau d'Awkward. She heckled the band to set up faster, hoping it would distract from his prickly presence.

Gia noticed Patrice's rudeness. "Hello, Paul."

"Gia," he nodded.

"Sorry for intruding," she smiled, gesturing to the wings.

"Unfortunately, it's not my building," was his curt reply.

Aleli and Pam appeared. "Hey! You guys thirsty?"

"Parched!" squealed Patrice.

"Lars has the refreshments, let's go!"

Aleli and Pam dragged them away. Patrice followed happily, but when Gia turned to bid Paul goodbye, she noticed an odd expression on his face. It looked a lot like hurt.

"Ladies," said Lars graciously as they arrived in front of his apartment and immediately handed them cups of vividly pink gin and pomelo juice. Inside, the unit was packed with UMC members jostling, singing and laughing. They were on the second floor—Apartment H1—a few doors down from Migs' place. Gia watched for any sign of Migs as Patrice chatted with Lars.

"How'd you like the gig?" he asked.

"It was great!" said Patrice.

"I'm not sure but Lars seemed extra-inspired tonight," said one of the UMC members whom Patrice didn't know by name. Hoots and cheers followed, plus a sly smile from Lars.

"I'm just extra happy," he joked, to more cheering from the crowd. Patrice was glad for the dimness that hid her blushing.

Soon she was inside, in the middle of a drinking circle, with Lars on her left and a gangly guy in the center doling out shots from a bottle of cheap tequila. "No chasers!" he screamed at her. "Just whistle!"

Patrice took a shot, grimaced through her burning throat, and whistled.

"Attagirl!" yelled Lars, patting her on the back—and letting his hand rest there.

The shots made their rounds to everyone in the apartment. Gia politely refused, pretending to drink from a prop cup of gin pomelo. Too quickly the tequila bottle emptied, a hat was placed on the floor for people to chip in money, and with reassurances that alcohol was on its way, the drinking circle broke up. The Alta girls decided to get some air at the hallway.

"Bad trip!" said Pam. "We're out of alcohol. You guys are so cheap!"

"You just drink too much!" a yell answered from inside.

"I'm buying, I'm buying," grumbled Lars good-naturedly as he left.

"Oy, you two," said Aleli to Patrice and Gia. "You know those Phi Delta Phi guys at the end of the hall, right? Maybe they can spare a small bottle of gin or something?"

Gia looked like she wanted to disappear.

"Look at them," Aleli pressed, jerking her head towards Migs' apartment. A group of fratmen and sorority girls hung out by the banister, everyone clutching bottles of beer or cups of punch. "They look pretty rich to me. I'm sure a bottle of gin's no biggie to them."

"Come on!" cried Pam. "Before my buzz dies!"

"Look, if you're *dyahe* or whatever just bring me along, introduce me to your friends and I'll do all the begging. I have no shame," said Aleli.

"Alcoholic!" some guy shouted.

"At least I'm resourceful, no?" Aleli shot back. "And you're going to drink it anyway!"

Gia turned to Patrice. "This is so embarrassing."

Maybe it was the tequila, but Patrice found it the opposite of embarrassing. "No Gia!" she cried happily. "This is the perfect excuse for you to see Migs. Reconnect!"

"To beg for gin?"

"Trust me! It's a party! It's cool!"

"Well girls? Are we mooching or what?" Aleli threw her arms around them and marched them down the hall.

Fortunately, the first person they encountered was Jon. As the frat president and unofficial ambassador, it was his duty to be polite and welcoming, even though some of the fratmen looked puzzled at their arrival. The cattier sorority girls, who'd followed Marga from downstairs, threw dirty looks and *what are they doing here?* sneers at each other.

"Gia! Hello!" he said. "And hi, uhm…"

"Patrice," she answered, too tipsy to be offended. "Hi Jon! Great party huh? Have I introduced you to my dormmate, Aleli?"

Jon grinned as politely as he could as Aleli launched herself on him, pumping his hand in a car salesman sort of way. "Why hello, Jon!" she said. "I see you all the time but I believe we've yet to be introduced—what a shame, really, I mean, we're in one big happy University after all…" She prattled on, maneuvering him inside the apartment, leaving Patrice and Gia to fend for themselves in a potentially hostile environment. It took longer for Patrice to realize just how, despite the forced politeness from the fratmen, uncomfortable their presence really was. She was just about to agree with Gia, who had been whispering constantly that they "leave—NOW" when Paul squeezed past the mass of bodies at his door and handed them two cups of punch.

Patrice was so taken aback that it fell on Gia to respond. "Thanks so much Paul. I'm so sorry, I know we're intruding and you'd much rather rest—"

He waved away her apologies without meeting her eyes.

Silence for a few moments.

"So how are you coping?" asked Patrice, who'd recovered her nerve.

"Coping?"

"With the noise. The music. The *dancing*."

He thought for some time. Patrice began to wonder if he was just going to stand there, like a robot crashing, when he finally said: "I know I sometimes come off as very stand-offish." He cleared his throat. "It's just that I'm. I'm not really good at. Socializing. Small talk, parties, things like that—it's just not me."

"Well, how does anyone ever get good at anything?" said Patrice. "Practice. Maybe you should practice, then."

He pressed his lips together and said, "Maybe."

"I think I get it now," said Patrice, the bright tequila buzz still exerting itself.

"Get what?"

"I always wondered how someone like you'd be friends with Migs," she said as Paul watched her mouth. "But then I remember. Boyhood friends. Maybe you weren't so crap at socializing then." She nudged her head toward the door, where Migs stood and Marga whispered a continuous stream at his ear. Unnoticed by Patrice, Gia went pale, her heart hammering. "You played with toy cars, maybe you tortured a frog together. There you go. Friends."

"Something like that." He considered her for a moment and then leaned closer. "Listen. Do you want to—"

"Hey!" Lars suddenly appeared, put his arm around Patrice, and pulled her close. "I was looking for you. Tequila's ready."

Paul and Lars exchanged tense glances.

"Paul," Lars said, cocking an eyebrow and a barely concealed smirk. He stroked Patrice's ponytail, lifting it away from her neck. She felt warm tingling from her scalp to the soles of her feet.

Paul spun on his heel and entered the apartment without another word. Aleli, narrowly missing a collision, stumbled out at the same time, apparently after inducing the people inside into a drinking game, because they patted her on the back and mussed her hair as she left, yelling, "You're the bomb Aleli!" and "Come back tomorrow!"

They followed Lars down the hall back to his apartment. But instead of entering, Gia tapped Patrice on the shoulder. "I need to go."

"What—Gia, come on!"

"No thanks Patits, I'm just so tired…" she trailed off, looking downcast.

Patrice ushered Gia to a more private corner. "What's wrong?"

She hesitated and then, "I saw *him*, Patrice. He looked straight at me and—and then he looked away. It was as if I didn't exist."

"Gia, come now, maybe he didn't really—"

"No, Patrice, he saw me, I knew he did. Our eyes met, we stared at each other for a long time. I raised my hand to wave and he stopped himself from waving back. Then he looked away."

"Don't worry, Gia, I'll talk to him, I'll—"

"No," she said, resigned and angry. "Don't bother. You said it yourself, if he ignores me than he's a jerk who isn't worth it. I'm glad I found out sooner rather than later."

"But G—"

"Listen, I'm not feeling very well. Would you mind if I went home?"

Patrice wanted very much to comfort her friend, to convince her to enjoy the party. But the hurt look in her eyes and the steel in her posture clearly said she needed to be alone. Patting Gia on the shoulder and resolving to get to the bottom of this, she bid her good night.

Patrice thought she saw her roughly wipe her cheek as she left.

"Where'd your friend go?" asked Lars, leading her to the stairwell.

"She was tired." He handed her a plastic cup of 'margarita'—some concoction of juice and tequila by one of Lars' friends. It was vile, but Patrice didn't mind. She was too busy being charmed by Lars, whose full attention was on her, and who was joking about her maniacal varsity coach. He had known the coach as a freshman, when he had tried out for the team himself. But music was a stronger draw than sports. "I hope that doesn't offend you?" he laughed.

"Not at all," she said. "We can't all give in to our passions."

"We could," he said with a naughty grin, "but it'd be messy, don't you think?"

A couple of people told Lars they were calling it a night. As he made his goodbyes, Patrice took a moment to steady herself. Her heart was beating fast and her head swam— maybe it was the tequila—but suspected Lars had much to do with it too. He was charming and sweet and good with people and talented, all the things she thought she liked in a person.

They spoke some more of other general topics for some time, before Lars, taking a meaningful pause, asked her how she knew Paul Dalmacio.

"He's my classmate," she said. "ENG 5." Mumbling, she added: "Irritating guy."

Lars looked relieved. "You think so?"

She smirked. "Ugh. He never says anything unless it's to belittle someone or something. Arrogant Applied Math nerd."

"You're one of the few people who'd say that, you know," said Lars. "Most people think of him as this smart leader-type. I think people mistake his silence for deep thinking."

"Oh?" said Patrice, eyebrow arched. "And what do *you* think?"

"I think he's full of it," said Lars. "Then again, I've known him longer than most people."

This piqued Patrice's curiosity. "Really?"

"He was my classmate in high school. For a year."

Patrice was astonished.

"We moved around a lot when I was younger," he explained. "I went to his school when I was, oh, fifteen, sixteen, around third year."

"And how was he then?"

"Pretty much the way he is now," said Lars. "Quiet all the time, unapproachable, a snob. You know how dumb some people can be, when they meet a guy like that? They automatically think there's something about him that might be 'deep', so they hang around him, inflating his ego some more."

Patrice thought that sounded pretty much like Paul, but still tried to inject bit of fairness into the conversation. "I think his attitude is annoying, but harmless, really."

Lars smiled ruefully. "I thought so too, but I learned I was wrong—the hard way." He seemed to dwell deeper on the topic for a few moments.

"Yes, we were friends—once."

She looked at him, surprised.

He chuckled without much humor. "It amazes me now, but yeah, back then, we were close. I think he liked to hang around me because I 'softened' his personality a bit, you know? Made him more approachable. Friendlier. I admit I was one of the people fooled into thinking he was a deeper person than he really was."

Patrice did not know what to say but was eager for the story to continue.

"I had a lot of friends; him, a few. One of the girls in class became close to both of us." He looked away and seemed pained. "Angel."

Patrice tried to guess what followed. "And you both fell in love with her, is that it?"

Again Lars laughed bitterly. "I wish it had been as simple as that. Yes, I liked her, very much. She was smart, and athletic. Funny, too. You kind of remind me of her. But she liked Paul. Always did, since fifth grade, she said. Of course, what could I do? I was her friend, I was Paul's friend. I kept my feelings to myself and let them…do whatever they wanted."

"What happened?"

"Well, at first everything was nice and peachy. They became a couple and everybody loved them. What a perfect pair—smart, studious Paul, popular Angel. They were a big hit at the prom."

"Let me guess: you had to play the sweet song they slow-danced to?" joked Patrice.

"Bingo," smiled Lars. "*Is It OK If I Call You Mine*?" He shuddered. "I never want to remember that, ever!"

"And then…?" prompted Patrice.

"And then I found out it wasn't so perfect after all. Angel would come to me, crying, saying Paul was ashamed of her. That he never brought her to meet his family. That he would never introduce her to his friends outside school. That he never listened to her and thought she was dumb. That she felt she was never good enough for him."

Patrice shook her head. "I can imagine that."

"One day, we had a group project together. We stayed over after class to work on it. I'd just gone to the canteen to get soda for us. When I came back to the classroom…I…" he broke off.

"What happened?"

"They didn't notice me. They were arguing. I don't know or remember what about. All of a sudden he—he drew his hand back and he…he shoved her."

Patrice gasped, clasping her hands to her mouth. Lars forearms tensed, as if remembering the pain of that moment.

"He just pushed her, Patrice. Just, *boom*, like that. My mind went dark. I just ran in there. The next thing I knew, I was sitting on top of him, he had a cut above his eye and a split lip. A janitor was pulling me away."

"Oh, my gosh," she said, her hands still against her mouth.

"Can you guess what happened next?" he asked. She shook her head.

"I got kicked out. Naturally."

"No—!"

"Oh, you know, we had the usual meeting at the Principal's Office, but it was for nothing. Angel didn't want to talk about it and made me swear I wouldn't tell what I saw because she didn't want to be humiliated. And when you have a kid like me—dad's overseas, transferring schools every few years, a reputation for liking 'Satanic rock music'—against Paul, who was quiet and got good grades and very rich—well, who's going to believe that I didn't start it?"

"That's just so awful!" cried Patrice.

"It was a month before the school year ended, too. My mom had to go there and beg them to just let me take the finals. She promised that I wouldn't show my face in class, I'd do the exams in the Principal's Office, I'd transfer schools. Thankfully, they took pity on a screw-up like me. I was able to take the final exams, passed, went to some tiny provincial high school that one of my mom's uncle's friends owned just so I could finish senior year. And thankfully, despite all of that, I was still able to graduate with good grades and get myself here. But if Paul would have had his way, I bet I wouldn't be at the University now."

"How can you stand living so close to him?" she said, full of indignation.

He shrugged. "Well, I'm a big enough man to realize that all that's kid's stuff. It's in the past."

"That doesn't make it right!"

"It doesn't, but what can you do? As long as your grades make it, the University doesn't really care about your 'good morals and right conduct,' plus I can't prevent him from living here, can I? Anyone who can pay on time has a right to rent a place at U.S.A. Besides, if he has a problem with me, *he* can move, or he can do something about it, if he's man enough." He put his arm around her. "So, on that count, I have nothing to worry about."

She was furious. She had always thought Paul to be an unpleasant, conceited man, but she had never suspected just how awful he could really be. To put a hand on a girl— someone he claimed to love! It was despicable, cowardly, evil. Then there were his actions after…He considered Lars a friend, yet stood by and did nothing when his former friend was forced from school.

She chalked it up to a mixture of pride, malice and cowardice. "I always knew there was something about him that I didn't like," she muttered.

"What's the matter?" asked Lars, pulling her closer. "Don't think about that anymore. I just wanted you to know the kind of people your friend is friends with."

She looked sharply at him. "What do you mean? Do I need to know anything about Migs?"

"Migs is a good guy," said Lars quickly. "I don't know him personally, but everyone says he's cool. Not very much like a fratman at all."

"Yeah," said Patrice thoughtfully. "But you have to wonder how a person like that can really be so close with someone like Paul without having some sort of attitude problem himself. He said they were childhood friends— you'd think he'd know about his friend's temper."

"I think that Paul can make himself very well-liked if he thinks the crowd's worth it," said Lars. "Migs is also a rich kid, plus he's Phi Delta Phi. Do you know how well-connected that frat is? Without being a member, without being hazed or going through initiation, Paul will have the advantages of the frat alumni network once he graduates, and all for being friends with Migs. Say hello to business connections, resume references, the works."

She shook her head in disgust. "It's so weird that more people don't see through his act!"

"Like I said, sometimes people *want* to be deceived."

They sat together in silence for a few minutes. Patrice couldn't think of anything else but her discovery of Paul's faults that she was unable to join any other conversation. Thanking Lars, she excused herself and went home, where, after a long shower, she fell into a confused and agitated sleep.

Chapter 7

Patrice awoke like she had been punched in the gut. Her conversation with Lars still bothered her all throughout the weekend, even through her game, so that the coach subbed her out after the first half. Her performances was, in his words, disastrous.

There was another game coming up on Wednesday, which she was determined to prepare for. Unfortunately she had slept through her customary morning jog. And worst of all, since it was a Monday, it meant that her first class was ENG 5. *With Paul*. And today would be consultations with the instructor on their paper, which was to be passed on Wednesday. She had received his email with his half of the paper a few days before the party at U.S.A., but had wanted to clarify a few things with him to get the conclusion into more cohesive shape. She hoped Nadia could help them hash it out since she wasn't particularly keen on probing Paul on the specifics of his orphan-trauma. Oh no, not at all.

After a hasty breakfast and spending a long time in the bathroom envisioning what she would say to him, Patrice rushed to class, her heart inexplicably pounding in her chest. She entered the classroom, nodded at Paul (without meeting his eyes) and got sucked into a one-sided conversation with Bit-Bit. Nadia entered and called the class to order; pairs of students came one after the other to her desk, showing their outlines. Bit-Bit was now engaged with her groupmate, and Patrice, trying but still incapable of making any conversation with Paul, settled for chewing her lip and studying her fingernails.

"Patrice Reyes and Paul Dalmacio," said Nadia.

Clutching the outline of their paper, Patrice warily approached the desk. Paul, however, cut in and strode ahead of her.

"OK, guys, what do you have for me?"

"Actually," said Paul, before Patrice opened her mouth to speak, "I decided to complete my paper."

Patrice mouth dropped open.

"Oh, so you and Patrice finished early?" smiled Nadia.

"No. I mean I completed my paper," he said, handing it over and not looking at either of them. "I have several exams coming up this week and decided it was best to complete it ahead of time, and since I could not consult with my groupmate—so, um, here's the paper."

Nadia counted the pages, disbelieving. But his submission met all her requirements. "Well then. Since it seems that this is in order, I guess that means you'll be doing your own paper as well, Patrice? Do you have something for me?"

Patrice racked her brains to come up with something while Paul slipped back to his seat. Because her outline was based on the "he said, she said" concept she was supposed to do with Paul, she floundered her explanation and Nadia became increasingly annoyed with her, remarking, "ENG 5 may 'just' be an elective course but if you don't take this seriously I won't pass you either."

Heart pounding and visions of a big red "5" (the University's failing grade) scrawled on her class card, she sat out the rest of the class in a barely-controlled nervous fury.

Soon as the bell rang, Paul strode out the classroom without a backward glance. Unable to contain herself, she followed.

"Hey! Hey you! PAUL DALMACIO!" she screamed.

He stopped and turned, his eyes unable to hold her gaze for long.

"What the *hell* are you doing?" she demanded, dropping her notes and pushing his shoulder.

He bent to pick them up. "Patrice—I—"

"You are really evil," she spat, grabbing the notebook back. "You know—you *know*—that I'm here on scholarship. I've told you that if there's anything I don't mess with, it's my academics. So, what, you want me to fail ENG 5? Get me kicked out of school too?"

He looked puzzled and a crease appeared between his eyebrows. "That wasn't my intention at all—"

"Then *what*?!" she exploded, oblivious to the looks of the people of The Org, in front of whose table-and-bench *tambayan* she decided to have her big blow out. "*Why* leave me hanging on this project if you don't want me to fail?" A tear suddenly sprang from her right eye, and she brushed it away furiously.

He reached out to her face but she stepped away from him.

"Patrice—"

"Don't you freaking dare!" she said. "I thought you were harmless. Annoying, but harmless. Lars was right about you!"

At the mention of Lars' name, Paul suddenly straightened. Through gritted teeth, he said, "And you believe anything he says?"

"Of course I do!" she said. "You treated him awfully, and you're doing the same to me!"

"You're wrong," he said, quietly. Noticing the stares and titters of passers-by, he pulled her away to a space partially hidden by a disused blackboard and the building's photocopier. The crease between his eyebrows deepened, and a trace of guilt—or was it something else?—glimmered in his eye. "I'm not doing this to torture you, Patrice. I just— I can't work with you." She opened her mouth to argue but he pressed on before she could get a word in. "I can't concentrate when I'm with you. You said you care about your grades. I do too, even if it's 'just' an elective. I thought it would be better this way…we could do our own thing, and I wouldn't be distracted."

"What the—we can always email, you don't have to—"

"I can't work because I have—I'm having these—these feelings for you."

The words greeted Patrice like a slap in the face. "What?" she asked, feeling slow and stupid.

"I like you, Patrice. A lot." He seemed to be trying to reign himself in, physically clamping down. "But you seem to be interested in…other things. And I don't want to always be around someone who —"

"Doesn't feel the same way about you?" finished Patrice. "That's nice. 'It's useless finishing my paper with Patrice since I can't get in her pants anyway!'"

"That wasn't —" spluttered Paul, raising his voice for the first time.

"—and so you decide to leave me hanging instead, is that it? Who cares if Patrice fails the course, my poor ego might be wounded!"

"Patrice, listen—"

"No!" She shoved her notebook against his chest. It didn't hurt much and only smushed her notes, but he still winced. "I wish I had never met you, Paul Dalmacio!" Then she spun on her heel to cheers and hoots of approval from the watching members of The Org.

"FAMAS awards, mother!" yelled Claude, fanning himself at the head of the *tambayan*.

"Oh shut up!" called Patrice without turning or breaking her stride.

Paul, meanwhile, oblivious to the hubbub surrounding him, clutched the spot near his heart where he was hit with the notebook and slowly, his shoulders hunched and his face clouded with worry, trudged back to the Math building.

Patrice worked furiously on her paper the whole day, even going so far as to skip lunch and *merienda*—something that shocked Gia, who often found Patrice with a piece of bread or *hopia* stuck in her mouth. Not even the din and crash of Aleli's band practicing in the patio could rouse her from her work.

But soon her stomach won over and, after surpassing the ten-page mark on her paper, she saved her work on Gia's laptop and reluctantly went downstairs for dinner.

"Hey there, Miss Studious," said Aleli, who was sitting on the kitchen sink and eating *chichacorn* out of a small plastic bag.

"Hey," mumbled Patrice, who just discovered with despair that all that was left of the night's *menudo* dinner was tomato sauce, bits of potato and carrot and a few sad pieces of liver. She spooned this sad mulch over a bowl of rice, ignoring the protests of her stomach at the meager meal.

"So serious!" said Aleli. "Why don't you join us outside? We're just packing up. It's super hot in here anyway."

Patrice's back was indeed moist with the stifling humidity in the kitchen, and the thought of the breezy patio—where Lars waited—seemed like a good idea. *I can stay for five minutes* only, she told herself. *That paper will not finish itself.*

She followed Aleli out the door, where she found Pam packing up and Deenie cross-legged on the floor, oblivious to the tiny shorts riding up her crotch, staring raptly as Lars twirled drumsticks in front of her.

"Hi!" Lars greeted as soon as he noticed Patrice. "I was hoping to see you here."

"Hey, Patrice!" trilled Deenie. "You missed their set. It was awesome!"

"Deenie, we were just practicing," said Pam. "You're so *exagge.*"

"But you guys are so good!" Deenie was practically quivering with excitement.

"Hey, Lars," Patrice smiled despite her exhaustion. "Can't stay. It's been a long day. I have this monster paper to do." And then, "No thanks to that ex-friend of yours."

"What did he do?" he asked, helping Pam stow equipment away.

"Nothing unexpected." She stifled a huge yawn.

"Whoa," said Pam. "Careful or you'll unhinge your jaw, woman."

"I'm just *so* exhausted. And I still have five more pages to do!"

"Why don't you take a break?" smiled Lars. "Have a beer. On me." He placed his arm around her and began maneuvering her to the gate.

"That's a first," said Aleli, with a snort. "You never buy Pam and me a drink."

"That's 'cause you two are *tomadors,*" he said, pulling Patrice. "I'd go broke in an hour!"

"Lars," Patrice protested, wriggling away from him. "I can't go."

"Of course you can," he smiled, pulling her once again. "Come on!"

"No. Lars," she said, this time more forcefully. "I need to finish my paper tonight so I can pass it to Nadia tomorrow morning because I'm missing her class on Wednesday—"

"Come on Patrice, it's just one beer," he said, squeezing her against him. "Live a little. Let your hair down."

Although she did feel a slight flush of pleasure when he tugged her ponytail, she had to decline. "I'm really, really sorry, Lars. I'm just tired and I have a million things to do. Maybe next time?"

Lars still smiled but it seemed forced, less warm somehow. He shrugged. "Your loss. Rain check then?"

"Soon as this nightmare Hell Week is over," said Patrice. "I gotta go."

He put his hand over his heart. "Aw. You broke it."

"You'll survive," she said.

"What about you, Deenie? You up for it?"

"Yes!" Deenie squealed in excitement. "Let's go!"

Chapter 8

Patrice's stomach was in knots. It was always like this before a big game. This was going to be the last one in their bracket. They won their first match, lost their second game against St. Clements but, despite Patrice's sub-par performance, won the next one against Laguna Tech's injury-riddled squad. If they swept this, they would get into the semis. That they would have to face St. Clement's again at some point since St. Clement's had already won all their three games was certain, but Patrice pushed that thought from her head.

Today was about finishing second in their group, securing a spot in the quarters, and the Blessed Mother College squad's 5-4-1 formation, scary sweeper, and veteran goalkeeper. She would *not* think about that jerk Paul Dalmacio or pine for Lars Capili. Patrice bit the inside of her cheek and swallowed a lump of nerves.

Kitty drew them all in a circle. "We can do this, guys. Yes, they're full strength, but so what? We can take them. We are the head and not the tail. We are mighty!"

"Mighty!" the team screamed, their hands grasped together in the center of the huddle. Their coach appeared and gave last minute tips about the game, the opposing squad and how they would penetrate their defense. Before she knew it she ran down to the field with the rest of the starting 11 to begin the game.

This was what she liked best about football. It was like another part of her brain woke up and took control. Nerves, analyses, worries—they all fell with a dim clatter to the back of her mind, and all that mattered was the Present: this field, this ball, and the wind on her face as she raced past players. She was a machine that responded to angles and physics. Her body instinctively understood the flight path of the ball and curved her leg at just the right angle to make it sail towards Catch; moments later, without thinking, she folded into herself as the ball rocketed back towards her, trapping it in her chest and arresting its momentum so that it fell a few inches from her feet, and with her tongue firmly pressed in her cheek towards the direction she wanted to go (a habit she swore to unlearn, but never did) the ball danced with her as she drove it forward, moving past defenders and flicking it in a swift, grass-hugging pass to Kitty, who quickly and decisively put it away in the net.

Their first goal! She glanced at the scoreboard. Forty minutes had already passed, a blur. Kitty jumped on her back, yelling; the rest of the team piled on top of them cheering madly, and then the whistle blew again. "Don't let it be over," she found herself thinking. "Don't let the first half stop." She knew that once the half-time whistle blew and they returned to their assigned bench for the fifteen-minute break she would feel the pain, the old ache in her right heel, the spot near her rib where Blessed Mother's striker clattered into her not ten minutes ago, but now she ran and now she felt alive like nothing she ever knew.

Half-time came and went; true enough a bruise bloomed blue and yellow on the curve of her rib, but she didn't care about it now. On and on they came, her team, relentless, tireless, ruthless. She felt this game was theirs—they all did.

Sometimes when you played it felt like all the pieces fell in the right place and the ball obeyed your every command. Sometimes it was the total opposite—no matter how much you struggled and did your best, all the forces of nature were against you and your best attempts were thwarted by some random rule of physics. It was why athletes were so superstitious, Patrice thought as she tackled a winger; it was why Anette the goalkeeper spat on her gloves and clapped them three times every time she had to face a penalty kick and Kitty had a blue kinetic tape cross on her hip and Catch had a lucky sports bra. You prepared as much as you could, but the game obeyed its own rules and followed its own destiny.

Today, the game was on their side. April Hizon, a muscular sophomore who had just made it to the first team that semester, scored a terrifying header off a corner kick—a shot so forceful and strong it rattled the crossbar and the whole Blessed Mother team. After that it was just a matter of keeping them shaken, and Patrice and the rest of the University's defenders had fun with sliding tackles and harassing their opponents when they possessed the ball. At ninety-four minutes, the final whistle blew and it was all over. Two-zero, and the University was into the semis.

There was the elation of victory, a balloon of pride swelling in Patrice's chest, and the sweet fatigue of a game well played.

The team bus pulled up in front of Alta's gate at a little past one in the morning. They had rented a party house with a pool that evening to celebrate with beer, noodles, roast chicken and a late moonlight swim. Now they were all scrubbed up, skin slightly chalky from the warm hot spring-fed water, and Patrice felt as if she were still floating. It was a queer feeling, but pleasant. Mingled exhaustion of tired muscles and soaked skin, and the slowly leaking elation of winning.

Feeling more than ready for bed, she bid her teammates and coach goodbye and blundered into the patio—where her heart suddenly and decidedly plunged to her knees.

There on the garden set, beside Miss Alya and her ever-present cup of black coffee, was Paul.

"Patrice." Miss Alya inclined her head. "Got a text from coach. Congrats on your game."

"Thanks," she stammered.

"Paul here saw it and says you were very good."

"Uh. Thanks?"

"His friend Jon was here too, but he left a while ago." She stood, favoring them with a small half-smile, and went inside. "Do lock the door when you're done, Patrice."

She watched Miss Alya leave with nerves suddenly and decisively awake, alert, alive.

"It's true, you had a great game," said Paul.

She sank onto the seat opposite him, the gym bag falling with a muffled *whump* at her feet. "So you really did watch?"

"Yes. With Jon. We checked it out. Caught the last half." He coughed. "Anyway. We got back around seven." He cleared his throat again and turned to watch a noisy motorcycle progress down the street. "I've been here since then. I want to talk to you."

"What about?" she asked.

His thumbs must have been extremely fascinating. "I realize you didn't take my decision about the paper in the best way possible, and that you brought up things about a person in my past that I felt were…untrue. And I wanted to explain things to you."

"You bet I didn't take it 'in the best way possible,'" scoffed Patrice. As his face fell, she added, "Well, go on then. You're here. Explain."

It took him some time to compose his thoughts and as he tried to do it, his gaze wandered all over the place. When it did sometimes land on her it was a confused, agitated sort of expression she did not expect to see. Patrice found him suddenly vulnerable in that moment, like a child with a secret he couldn't blurt out. The lost orphan he once was.

What am I even thinking? This is Paul, the Applied Math jerk!

"Before I start I want to ask you to let me speak first and not interrupt," he began. "When I'm done talking, you can ask whatever you like, or, which is better for me, not ask at all. I'm not after us being the best of friends or anything like that. I just do not like being judged without being able to say my side of the story. Whether you believe me or not, I don't care. As I said, you can take what I say or you can choose to think me a liar. All that matters to me is that I did what I could to explain. Is that alright?"

She stared back at him. It figured his deal would be all "me man talk/you woman listen" but whatever, she was tired and if this would speed things up, then: "Fine."

"I won't repeat what I said about how I feel about you. I knew it was…*disgusting* for you, I understand. So let's forget I ever said that. But you mentioned how 'Lars was right' about me, and I've been dwelling on those words for a long time." He broke off and stared at a spot on the patio for several moments. True to their agreement, Patrice waited for him to speak.

"I say what's on my mind, Patrice. I don't speak up unless I have to, so when I do I make sure that what I have to say is honest. Yes, even what I told you after ENG 5. Not a lot of people appreciate it. Many call my bluntness a fault, but it's a promise I made to myself. I will not lie. Someone like Lars knows how to charm and butter people up—good for him. I'm not like that, I promise you." He paused to compose himself. "I don't know what Lars told you, but I think I have an idea. First of all, yes, I knew him. We were classmates in our third year of high school."

He smiled ruefully. "Pop Kid Lars, we used to call him. At school for a week and everybody loved him already. And why not? He could charm anyone, he played drums, he could do whatever sport you asked him to. It was a small high school—there were only sixty of us in the whole third year—and everyone was friends. Including us."

"There was a girl…" Patrice began, then clamped her mouth shut.

"Angel, yes," he said quickly. "His girlfriend."

Well this is news to me. She would keep her promise to be quiet till he finished, she reminded herself.

"I liked her too. We had been classmates since fifth grade and I always found her nice. But I could never work up the nerve to…you know, really get to know her, apart from school. And I was never popular. I was quiet and I had a few friends and even if we talked a bit we moved in different circles…Anyway, when I finally told myself that I would get it together and talk to her, well. Lars came along and they were going out within a week. But, you know. That happens. It's fine."

He cleared his throat. "But then our intramurals came along. There was cheering practice, and I had basketball practice too, and sometimes Angel would ask me if she could hitch a ride with me after cheering because at the time she and Lars weren't doing too well and she lived near my place. I brought her to her house a couple of times, and she told me things about Lars that made me —" He pushed at his hair forcefully and then looked straight at her. "He was too physical—if you get my meaning. We were in high school. She was a virgin. She wasn't ready. But he just kept pressuring her, and she got upset so she told him they needed to stop seeing each other for a bit." He broke off and ran his hands through his hair again, clearly agitated.

"I know this is coming off as talking shit and I can hear that. And I wish it didn't. But it's the truth. That was what happened." He cleared his throat again. Patrice noticed a slight shake in his hand as it lay on his thigh. "So this was going on and one afternoon Angel said we would meet at our classroom after practice because she had some books to pick up. So after basketball I went there. And I saw them. And…and it wasn't very good." He paused for breath. "He had her pushed against the wall, Patrice. His hand was under her shirt. And she was whimpering and pushing. 'Please,' she kept on saying. And I heard him say, 'You want this. I know you do. You want this.' And she started to cry."

Patrice was speechless. She didn't know what to say, or what to think. She just wanted Paul to stop talking.

But he wasn't finished yet.

"When I heard that, something snapped inside of me. I don't speak up a lot or get in trouble and I prefer to keep to myself, but I couldn't see something like that and do nothing. I mean, I already kept out of it in spite of what she'd told me—but this, this was too much. I ran inside and pulled him off her and before I knew it I was kneeling on his chest slamming my fist on his face, and then someone was pulling me off him. It was our PE teacher, my basketball coach. Angel had called for him. Lars' face was a mess. I wanted to feel guilty about making his cheek swell like that but the truth is I couldn't care less." He fixed her a steady glare. "He deserved what he got, and to be honest with you every single day that I pass him by at U.S.A. I want to do it all over again. He's a prick. It was great when our principal read between the lines of what Angel said about that afternoon and kicked him out of school. But it was a sorry day when he got accepted here. "

There were a few seconds of silence as Patrice absorbed what he said. "Are you finished?" she asked.

"Yes."

"I don't know what to say, Paul," she said. "Do you want me to say that I think it's awesome you beat up Lars one time in high school?"

"I don't want you to say anything. I just want you to know the truth."

"Which is conveniently opposite what he told me."

"I don't care what he said. I just want to be honest and truthful and let you know the kind of guy you—you like."

"What is it about him that pisses you off so much, Paul?" said Patrice. "Is it because he finds it in his heart to be nice to people? To greet them? To be sociable? That he wants to be liked? Would you admire him so much more if he were like you?"

He stood up quickly. "And what am I like?"

"Arrogant. And pig-headed. And aloof. Like you're *so* much better than everyone else. Heaven forbid that Paul Dalmacio should speak and the whole room not clap! And—and you're selfish!"

"Selfish?" he thundered.

"Yes, selfish!" she shot back. "Like this whole ENG 5 thing—doing the paper on your own because you can't work with me? Did it ever occur to you that you're not the only person who would be affected by that? Did you ever pause to think that, hm, maybe my groupmate Patrice has a lot going on right now, like, I don't know, a freaking important football game on which her scholarship depended, and maybe I should give her fair warning before hijacking our project so that she doesn't have to spend all Monday writing for nine hours straight just so she could pass that freaking paper?"

He dropped his gaze, looking like he'd been slapped.

"And what about your friend, Migs?" Patrice was unable to contain herself. "You're *surprised* that I called you selfish? Well, if you cared about your friend more you'd tell him what a bonehead he is to *my* friend."

Paul looked puzzled. "What are we talking about again?"

That night of the mid-term party, the night of begging-for-gin-at-Migs'-apartment flashed before Patrice's eyes. She felt annoyed at being reminded of the awkwardness of that evening, which made her even more irritated that Paul seemed to forget the whole thing.

"Migs and Gia!" she yelled. The low window beside Patrice's chair, which belonged to Aleli and Pam's shared room, creaked open. "S'that you Patrice?" a sleepy voice called out.

"Sorry, sorry, I'll keep it down," Patrice answered. When the window creaked shut, she started whispering at Paul, "You know very well that Migs likes Gia—all those mornings you two hounded my jogs, and him all 'Gia this' and 'Gia that'—so what happened now? Why isn't he talking to her? You let Marga talk him into thinking something awful about her, didn't you? I hope you're happy."

"Wow, and I'm *arrogant*?" Paul hissed back. "Who's arrogant now? You think Migs can't make up his mind about your friend? You think he needs a girl like Marga to tell him what to think? Migs liked Gia, that's true, but your friend doesn't like him back."

"What?" cried Patrice. She waited for someone to tell her to keep quiet again. The night remained still, so she began, softly now, "How could you even say that? Gia likes him! Very much!"

"Well, she has a nice way of showing it," said Paul, restless, pacing again. "Sure she smiles at him and is nice and polite, but she's like that to *everybody*. She doesn't treat him any differently, so who can say if she feels anything for him?"

"But that's because she's shy! I've known her for three years, Paul, and she never reveals her true feelings to anybody. Migs was the first guy she's ever liked!"

He faced the street and wet his lips.

"Wait a minute," said Patrice. "You said this all to Migs before, haven't you? You convinced him she doesn't like him, didn't you? "

"So what if I did?" he shot back. "Migs asked for my advice, and I gave it to him. He's a family friend, an old friend, we're like brothers. Hiding the truth from him would only hurt him more. He wanted to know if I thought Gia liked him, and I told him what I thought. I thought she didn't. So maybe I was wrong, or maybe I was right, does it really matter?"

Patrice got to her feet. "It matters because you broke my friend's heart," she said, jabbing his chest with her finger. "I can't believe you, Paul. You stand there, proud of what you did. You aren't even apologetic. You might've ruined what could have been a good relationship between two people who liked each other, and you don't even care. And you wonder why I said you were arrogant and pig-headed and selfish!"

He made himself face her. His mouth scowled but… did she imagine it, but was that hurt in his eyes?

"You say that Migs is like a brother to you. Did you ever think that he values your advice, and that even if he believed in one thing he would convince himself of the opposite, because *you* said so? This is what I mean, Paul.

Your precious blunt 'honesty' means so much to you that you don't stop to think that other people get hurt."

He remained silent, listening to every word she had to say. She knew she had to stop, that she would soon cross an invisible line between them, but she was angry and tired and hurt, and she went on.

"You say you don't want to repeat what you told me after our class. That's good, because I don't want to hear it. Yet you come here, with your stories of Lars being some sort of sexual predator, thinking you can win me over by spreading sick stories about him? Lars is a better man than you could ever hope to be, and I will never in a million years ever think differently. You are the last guy in the world I would ever want to be with!"

"Enough," said Paul, his voice rough and ragged. "I've heard enough. I told you what I came to tell you, in all honesty and with my conscience clear, but you clearly have your own ideas. I really hope, for your sake, that all of them are right. But forgive me if, based on my experience, I don't have high hopes for that."

To get to the gate and leave he had to edge closer to Patrice, who blocked his way. Her jaw was set, but her heart began to thrum madly against her ribs as he brushed past her. His face in that moment—he suddenly seemed so lost and defeated, that for half a heartbeat Patrice inclined closer to him. But he moved away. "I am so sorry to have wasted your time," he said, trudging out Alta's gate.

It was half past two in the morning when she entered her room. She watched Gia sleep while Deenie snored at the other end of the room. Gia could never know how Paul cruelly denied her a chance at happiness. He was a mean, hurtful, unpleasant, proud man, she thought, easing into bed.

But all through the early hours of dawn, sleep would not arrive. Her conversation with Paul continued to play in her mind. She kept on seeing his face. Worried and anxious one moment, proud and set the next. How he ran his hands through his hair as if he could throw the discomfort of what he wanted to say in the same movement. How the story of Lars and Angel seemed to wrench painfully from his heart, like it was something that hurt him to share. How his hands shook as he told it. And she began to wonder if she had misjudged Paul after all.

Yes, he was proud, and yes, he was blunt. But was that such a bad thing? And could he have been telling the truth about Lars? When it came down to it, Paul was fanatic about being honest and only speaking the truth—to the point that he came off as irritating and ill-mannered. A man who would risk being disliked just so he could be true to his principles wouldn't make up such an elaborate story about Lars, would he?

And what about Lars? How could she say that he was a better man than Paul? She had a crush on him, that was true, but she didn't know him as well as she would have liked. He *was* awfully flirty. And Paul's story, like a dark mirror image, seemed to match Lars' on relevant details. How could that be possible when neither of them talked about it?

The only thing she knew for sure was that she was confused. And when sunlight slowly leaked through the windows and the day came upon them, she began to dread going up to ENG 5 and facing Paul once again. Not now. Not after that night.

"I shouldn't have bothered," she told herself later, that morning, in class. The seat beside her was empty. Nadia just told the class what a shame it was that their token Applied Math classmate, despite submitting a really good paper, had decided to drop ENG 5.

Chapter 9

If there was a more miserable semester in her years at the University, Patrice didn't remember it.

Studying for the start of what would be a marathon of final exams, papers and projects as the semester wound down, Patrice paused in the middle of her notes on Jonathan Swift's *A Modest Proposal* and let her mind wander from the depressing topic of (satirically) eating babies as a cure for famine on to other sad-making things. Koko the parakeet chirped as Patrice slumped over the patio table, brooding over the odd turn of what she was sure to have been an awesome semester.

Gia was depressed, that Patrice knew for sure. Oh yes, she still did her best to be as pleasant and composed and good-natured as ever (Gia never *sulked*) but she liked to disappear into their room now, where Patrice would catch her staring out the window, clutching a pillow so tightly it seemed like she was trying to crush it.

But the worst thing was that, for the first time ever, Gia did not want to talk about it. They'd been as close as could be ever since they roomed together freshman year, telling each other everything, so Gia's newfound secrecy hurt Patrice. If she was honest with herself, it was because she was guilty: deep inside, she knew, she was complicit in Gia's heartbreak. Maybe if she wasn't so hell-bent on hanging out with Lars she would've noticed what was going on with Migs and stopped pushing her friend to go out that night, to that ill-fated trip to H-5, saving Gia from the embarrassment of Migs' rejection.

She had to make it up to Gia, somehow. She didn't know how or why, but she needed to do this for her friend. But at the moment, all she could do was wait for her to heal and appear ready to *accept* her help.

"Hey Patrice!" said Deenie, bounding out the door in a tank top and flouncy miniskirt. She stopped a moment to check her reflection on the window. "Seen Pam or Aleli anywhere?"

"No, Deenie."

"Oh. Well, if you do, tell them I'm at U.S.A.? And if my SOCSCI 1 groupmates come over, tell them—well tell them I'll schedule something again, all right?"

Patrice let a suppressed breath out her nose in one long, controlled exhale. "Sure thing, Deenie."

"Coolness!" she trilled, patting Patrice's head. "You sure you're OK? You look pale. You shouldn't study so much! Anyway. Take care now, bye bye then!"

Patrice watched Deenie practically skip down the street. Here was reason number two why this sem officially sucked: Deenie was on her way to see Lars.

She bumped her forehead on her notes, groaning. Over the past couple of weeks, Deenie had completely abandoned her quest to be super-besties with the Phi Gamma Chi sorority girls in favor of attending scruffy drinking-and-jamming sessions with the musicians and assorted hangers-on of UMC. It seemed that, while Patrice was off saving her grades from disaster, playing football and worrying about Gia, Lars and Deenie had discovered each other.

As far as she could tell from Deenie's excited little hints and showing off to her fellow freshmen, as well as Pam and Aleli's mumbled one-liners, it had all started when Deenie and Lars went out for a drink. The same drink that Patrice had, memorably, turned down. The two hit it off that very night—Aleli described them as "tonguing each other like when Jabba the Hutt *bo-shuda'd* that dancer"—and were practically inseparable afterward. Patrice had spent the next few days after her Blessed Mother match walking in on them canoodling in the patio, which was then inevitably followed by awkward "hi-hello" greetings.

Truth be told, though uncomfortable, Patrice didn't feel jealous. Not really, when she reflected on it. After the initial shock of seeing Deenie perched on Lars' lap and tickling him behind the ear, she realized that she really had no reason to feel bad. She and Lars hardly knew each other and had spent, at most, a couple of hours in each other's company. It was true that she had a crush on him and he had seemed to be into her, but after all, neither of them concretely suggested to each other that they might properly go out.

Besides, the more she thought about it, the more she realized that she and Lars would not have been a good match. Lars was freewheeling, happy-go-lucky; with the band he was frequently out attending or playing gigs—she wouldn't be able to keep up with the late nights. With her football and academic commitments, she wouldn't be the kind of girlfriend Lars seemed to require: Deenie often arrived back at the dorm very late, softly explaining that she had been out "to watch Lars" but that they needn't worry since she was chaperoned by Pam and Aleli. Patrice imagined herself in the same situation and shook her head. There was no way that she and Lars could be together without ending up fighting.

At the thought her face darkened as she remembered Paul's words to her on the patio and his horrible story of Lars groping his friend. No, it was just too awful to contemplate. Surely Paul was mistaken about the whole thing. Lars was quite the touchy-feely guy with Deenie, she'd noticed, but it seemed to be a natural, playful touchiness and not the unwelcome advances Paul described.

Just the same, Deenie's devotion to her new boyfriend did not go unnoticed. After a few afternoons Miss Alya started to make it a point to spend a few minutes (or an hour) gardening in or near the patio until the lovebirds got the hint and detached themselves from each other and Lars, inevitably, left. Even Mrs. Timbol of the ever-present matchmaking schemes had started commenting (ostensibly to herself, but everyone could hear it) that *some* lovely young ladies ought to play hard-to-get from time to time, since that made the prize "all the richer for the pursuer."

Patrice had rolled her eyes at that but Gia, to whom care of the freshman was entrusted, was worried. Isay had once let slip that Deenie missed a couple of her morning classes, so Gia took the time to speak to her "ward" and remind her that, however fun life at the University was, she was here to study and shouldn't forget her responsibilities. Deenie agreed and promised not to miss other classes, so Gia put off any mention of Deenie's love life in her replies to Deenie's mom's text messages.

Patrice put her notes aside and stretched. When it came down to it, she mused philosophically, there were girls like Deenie to whom romantic attachments came easy; they followed their hearts, got into sticky situations and got up to pursue other adventures. More power to them, but Patrice wasn't like that. She had too many responsibilities and, to be honest, she was much too afraid of being hurt to fling her heart open the way Deenie did.

Another sigh escaped her. If there was one consolation over this whole depressing season, it was that she got to re-do her disastrous ENG 5 paper. Nadia had spoken with her after one class and said that, while her original paper was OK, it could still improved, and if Patrice was up for it she could offer her a half-week's extension to get it right. Patrice took her up on it and the original, dismal 2.75 she had gotten was now elevated to a much more satisfactory 1.5.

The dorm's screen door flew open and out came Gia, rummaging in her purse. "Patrice!" she grinned.

"G!" Patrice answered with a smile. Was it wishful thinking or did Gia look, well, more herself than she had been these past few weeks? "Where you off to?"

"Patrice, you have to check your Facebook more often." Gia laughed, an easy, unaffected giggle that Patrice hadn't heard for the longest while. "Bit-Bit's been bugging us all to help out with their play."

"Ah, yeah, she corners me about that all the time," Patrice shook her head. "*How* do those guys find the time to do a play at the start of finals season?"

"Well, you do what you love, right?" said Gia. "So aren't you coming?"

"What?"

"Oh Patrice, she'd been messaging me non-stop that you and I *have* to be there. I thought you'd been getting them too?" she shook her head. "Come on, they're starting!"

"Starting what?" Patrice had no choice but to stow her notes inside and follow Gia out the gate. "So we're taking Raymundo, are we?" she remarked. "No more 'exercising' by taking the long way to the main gate?"

"What are you talking about, why'd anyone want to walk all the way to the main gate when we can get to the middle of campus in half the time?" said Gia airily.

Patrice laughed and followed her friend past computer shops, convenience stores, dorms and eateries, approaching the chicken-wire gate. Gia did seem more cheerful now, lighter, more at ease.

"OK, so I don't get it, G."

"Get what?"

She held her breath, weighed what she had to say, then chucked it out and decided to be blunt. "Right. I don't know if the ban on talking about this has been lifted so I hope I don't get the silent treatment again for bringing this up, but—are you, finally, OK?" Her voice took on more serious tone. "I've been worried about you all this time, and you hadn't been talking to me and I know you've been down about it and I've been so guilty—"

"Guilty?"

"—yes, because if I hadn't bugged you to go out that night and if I didn't push you to go to his apartment, I mean —"

"Patits, please. It's all right. I don't blame you for anything. Really." She grinned again and squeezed her friends shoulder. They stepped over Raymundo Gate's iron railing, crossed the street into campus and threaded their way through the low-roofed Management classrooms.

"Really? Because I still feel like a terrible shit, you know."

"Why would you say that?"

"Look, I know you say you don't blame me, but come on, if I hadn't been so crazy to hang out with Lars, none of this would've happened."

Gia's face darkened momentarily as they passed the back of the Humanities building. "Well, I'm not saying that *he* isn't a bit of trouble," and worry crossed her face as they both thought of Deenie, "but I don't blame anyone for what happened. As much as I'd like to cast it off somewhere, well, it's really between him and me, right? Somewhere along the way he—Migs —" (she seemed to psych herself up to say his name) "—*Migs* lost interest. And that's that. I'm sorry that it happened that way or that we didn't get a chance to speak afterwards because I would've liked to be friends— please don't look at me like that, I'm sincere! He's a nice guy and I think he's really great to talk to, but anyway, yes, that's my only regret. That we couldn't have ended as friends."

Patrice watched Gia say this speech. "So you're really fine? No more hard feelings?"

"So dramatic," she chided. "How can there be any hard feelings when there weren't any *other* feelings to start with?" She stopped abruptly at the foot of the bridge by the Co-Op.

"Look, you know me well enough to know that yes, it's true, I was disappointed. And yes, it's true, I did kind of brood about it for a while. But then, honestly, I got tired of being sad about it. I said to myself, 'Gia, you're being silly. Pull yourself together and get out there and just stop thinking about it.' And that's what I'm doing now. I can't pretend to understand what happened—although me getting gross and drunk at his place can't have helped things—but brooding won't help me understand it any better, would it? I've decided to be fine and I can tell you, Patits, that if I see him again I can be perfectly OK with him."

"Truly?"

"*Truly*," confirmed Gia. "I'll even go up to him and say hello and everything." She spun on her heels towards the Student Union building, Patrice hurrying to catch up.

"Well, I'm glad," Patrice said, reaching her friend by the ornamental pavilion, overgrown with broad-leafed shrubs and vines. "I couldn't stand see you sad. And you know, screw them—these guys who seem all interested one day and cold as ice the next." Seeing Gia's face fall she hastened to add, "I mean, it's nothing, compared to you and Migs, you know, I mean, Lars never, uh, *pursued* me in any way; it was all just…"

"Shocking," finished Gia. "You don't have to explain anything. I'd be shocked too if he flirted with me like that and then the next day started going out with Deenie. I just hope he's good for her. Older, I think, but maybe it's only because Deenie seems so young and eager—but I'm being silly. I mean, we're all in college, right? It's not like he's twenty-five or something."

Patrice grimaced, deeply uncomfortable. She watched Gia descend the steps to the Student Union building, towards the knot of students in the sunken courtyard, by the wide, dried up, Locsin-designed fountain. It was bordered by an odd, makeshift tent of black cloth sectioned off at the courtyard's other end. She debated if she should tell Gia what Paul had told her about Lars' past.

Hesitating at the lip of the stairs, she struggled, recalling the ugly story. Gia was now talking animatedly to some common friends, her face lit up and, for the first time, free from worry. She looked like she was making good on her promise to enjoy herself and forget about her heartache.

Patrice recalled Gia's anxiety on deciding whether to tell Deenie's mom about her daughter's missed classes and how she struggled before finally talking privately with Deenie about it first. She didn't want that anxious expression on her friend's face again.

Let her enjoy the night, Lord knows she deserves it, Patrice made up her mind as she went down. *Deenie did say that she would be taking her studies seriously after their talk, so maybe the whole delinquency thing was just getting carried away with her first sort-of serious college boyfriend. Besides, the semester's ending soon. If he's bad for her then the semestral break would cool them both off. No need to tell Gia about Paul's story and ruin her last few weeks of peace before classes ended. It would sort itself out.*

Yes, it would.

Friends greeted her as she joined them. "So anyone want to tell me what's going on?" she asked.

"Damn, girl, check your Facebook from time to time!" said a classmate.

"OK, in a nutshell, The Org's doing a play next week, right?" volunteered another girl in their group. "But one of their sponsors backed out so they need to make up a certain amount. So now they're doing a human auction to raise the funds."

"A what?" Patrice's eyes widened.

"It's like they auction off dates with their members," explained Gia. "I know, it sounds weird, but maybe it's fun!"

"Do you have an eye on any of their brods?" Patrice laughed, visions of Claude snapping his paper fan open coming to mind.

Gia joined in. "Silly; I just want to see what happens. You know The Org, they're full of tricks!"

Bit-Bit Velez emerged from the black tent, resplendent in a Cleopatra headdress and carried on the shoulders of two burly dudes. Two other members followed behind with a small component and a couple of speakers trailing a length of electric cord that extended all the way inside the Student Union building. Bit-Bit perched at the top of the disused fountain while some Org members plugged in an MP3 player and a mic into a speaker system. Beachy reggae music played as Bit-Bit stood and welcomed them.

"Good evening, darlings!" she said, blinking her false eyelashes and playing the role of society hostess to the hilt. "Tonight we have prepared a small, short, scrrrrr-umptious affair to help with our, er, benefactor issues. So NOT fabulous!"

Other Org brothers and sisters began emerging from the tent and mingled with the small crowd. Puzzled, Patrice watched them: they were relatively plain-clothed, though a few had paint streaks and glitter on their hands. If they were watching the whole thing with the crowd, then who would Bit-Bit be auctioning?

She found out soon enough. Bit-Bit had the crowd buzzing, and a few more onlookers, attracted by the commotion and at the sight of the pint-size Cleopatra sauntering on the fountain, began arriving from the open field opposite the building. Patrice nodded to April Hizon, who seemed to have just finished a jog with some friends and looked on with an expression that unmistakably asked, "What the hell is going on?"

"All right, now I know you're all excited to see me auction off my slaves for your amusement," Bit-Bit declared theatrically. "I must remind you that you can have them for one—and just one—night only. It is a date and you, my little darlings, must be on your best and proper behavior. I'll have none of my harem defiled, thank you very much! Furthermore all expenses on the date will be on your tab. So get ready to spend, darlings! You all know about the ATMs by the bookstore, right? I hope you have your cards ready: let's bring out the first slave!"

The two burly guys who had carried Bit-Bit up the stage—Patrice figured they must have been boyfriends of The Org's sisses—entered the black tent and emerged moments later with a shirtless man between them. The guy clambered up the fountain and faced the crowd—to a wave of shocked screams and hoots of joy. Zaldy Diaz, engineering senior, captain of the basketball team, and *shirtless*, stood with an embarrassed but game smile on his face, every muscle on his toned torso visible. Was that *body glitter* on his chest?

Bit-Bit gestured to him, encouraging the crowd to take the sight all in. "Let the bidding start!"

"Two hundred!" came an ear-splitting shriek to Patrice's right. One of her classmates had her hand in the air and was bobbing up and down excitedly.

"Two hundred?!" scoffed Bit-Bit. "What sort of loose change is this? Can't you do any better?"

"Five hundred!" came another shout, this time closer to the stage.

"Seven hundred!" another yell answered.

The bidding came fast and furious. Gia looked on with round, surprised eyes. "Goodness, they must be betting their week's allowance on him!"

"For a night with Zaldy, I'd gladly starve a month," came Claude's voice behind them.

"Hey, Claude!" said Patrice.

"Hey yourself, beeyotch," he said, scowling but with a teasing look dancing in his eyes. "I seem to remember that the last time we spoke you told me to shut up?" he snapped his fan open.

"Oh, Claude," said Patrice, grabbing his free hand and squeezing it against her. "You have to forgive me!"

"Yeesh!" he yelled, pulling it back to draw an invisible line between them. "Personal space, girl! Learn it, live it, respect it." This last line was delivered with a pout and an index finger touching Patrice's nose. Patrice cocked her hip and tossed her hair in response, giving her best bitchface, which finally succeeded in making Claude laugh.

On stage, Bit-Bit was readying another "slave" for bidding: a cute sophomore boy that they'd sometimes seen hanging out in the open benches in front of the Math building. She introduced him as Jacob Sy, BS Computer Science. April Hizon had her hand up even before Bit-Bit opened the bidding.

"Cute," Claude smiled approvingly before facing turning to Patrice, "Anyway, Patrice, I find it in my heart to forgive you, even if that was a really bitchy thing to do. Understandable, as you were having your FAMAS nomination reel moment, but still really bitchy."

"Sorry, Claude-Claude, I really am," Patrice mock-whined.

"Ugh, call me that again and I'll rescind my pardon!"

Up in front, April had won her bet, claimed the gold "date certificate" and was getting introduced to Jacob Sy. The two burly dudes were escorting another guy out of the tent, this time a Phi Delta Phi alumnus who had just graduated the previous semester.

Gia shook her head in disbelief. "I have to say, Claude, that this is the cleverest fundraiser you guys have come up with. This is fantastic!"

"Of course!" And he smiled magnanimously.

"How on earth did you get Bryan Samson to join the auction? I had the hugest crush on him when we were in PSY 101, freshman year."

"Bryan's internship just ended so he had a lot of free time. I gave him a call." At the incredulous looks of the two girls he started giggling. "Oh, okay, fine. I'd like to take credit and say it was all my natural charm, but in truth it was all thanks to—" Claude scanned the crowd for a few moments before finding his target "— that guy."

Patrice and Gia craned their necks to see where he was pointing and found their gaze directed to none other than Phi Delta Phi president, ferrety Jon Lee.

He caught their gaze and threaded his way towards them.

"*Jon Lee*?" Patrice gasped. "But why would he be interested in The Org's fundraising?"

"Beats me," said Claude, working his fan into a blur. "One day Bit-Bit and me were driving ourselves nuts trying to make up the budget shortfall and the next we were meeting with him and throwing ideas about how we could 'maximize his network.' He offered the, um, *resources* and we in The Org came up with the rest."

Jon was now a few paces from them and waving at Claude; Patrice stole a glance at Gia, who nodded almost imperceptibly and squeezed her hand to let her know she was fine.

"And here he is, the man of the hour!" said Claude, who hadn't noticed the pained, almost embarrassed expression flit through Jon's face. "We were just talking about all your help making this happen."

"Thanks, Claude, it's—it's my pleasure." Again, the odd, uncomfortable look. Patrice was puzzled, and from the glance that she exchanged with Gia, she wasn't the only one who caught it. Did he have some sort of complex about receiving compliments?

"Anyway, girls, it was nice to stay and catch up. Even with *you* Patrice," he turned on the disapproving diva act again, "but I think I'm wanted in the tent. Body glitter doesn't reapply itself, does it now?"

"Hi, Jon," Gia began, preventing an awkward silence now that Claude left.

"Gia, you're looking well," he replied. Gia thanked him as he continued, "We've missed you, you know; I hoped we'd see more of you around but —" he stammered at the look Patrice was giving him "I guess you're very busy with, uh, academics?"

"Ah, yes, that's right," said Gia.

They watched the stage. One of The Org's sisters, dressed in a feather boa and comically oversized pink shades, was tallying the money raised so far and was exhorting the crowd to bid more.

"So," said Patrice. "I hear this is all thanks to your help. Where are the rest of your brods?"

Jon sheepishly scratched the back of his head. "OK, girls, you have to promise not to tell anyone about this, but some of them are in that tent."

"For auctioning?" Patrice cried as he nodded. Gia suddenly looked stricken, and as the next auctionee stepped from the tent and up the stage, what she had silently dreaded faced them.

Migs Fuertes, in a white tank top and dark jeans, was up on stage.

Chapter 10

The crowd was going nuts and a bunch of girls were screaming like the fans in vintage Beatles concert footage. Bit-Bit drank it all in, relishing the crazed reaction. But what she said next surprised everybody.

"Now, now, settle down. I know you're all excited about our next slave. But darlings, it breaks my heart to tell you this, but I just received this note —oh, and it is such a disappointment!" Brandishing a stiff red envelope in the air and winking at Migs, she read: "'Dear Bit-Bit: We are sorry to say but a matter of great importance has just come up and we would like to apologize to the auction participants, but Migs Fuertes has been bought and pre-paid for...' Oh, my goodness darlings but this is huge!" she gasped. "'Please convey our regrets to everyone and if you would kindly ask the bearer of the gold date certificate to please claim Migs...' Well, all right! Let's see it then! Which of you greedy little divas deprived us of the chance of one night with Migs?"

At this, and to Patrice's utter shock, Jon reached into the back pocket of his slacks and slowly raised a glimmering gold certificate in the air. Gia looked on in disbelief and was even more mortified when Jon grabbed hold of her hand with his free one and raised it in the air.

The crowd went wild. Gia covered her face as she blushed a bright, furious red; some Org members began pulling her towards the stage. Bit-Bit laughed and shrieked while friends and classmates and strangers patted, congratulated and teased Gia as she made her way forward. Unable to wait, Migs jumped off stage, dashed through the crowd and caught Gia's hand in his. Whispering something to her ear—Gia seemed to tear up at this—he pulled her towards him and kissed her on the cheek.

The cheers were deafening. Around her, Patrice could make out: "Oh my God!" "That's so sweet!" "Awww, I'm so jealous!" "Lucky girl." "If only I had a Migs too!" and "I want to cry!" Bit-Bit was now wrapping things up: "On behalf of The Organization of Literature, Speech and Dramatics Majors, we'd like to thank you all for coming on such short notice! Grace informs me that we had just made the budget—we can't thank you all enough for your generosity. Thank you so much as well to Phi Delta Phi and friends—you guys are the best; thank you for being so game! See you all next week! Don't forget the three-day run of *Fourplay* at the DL Umali Hall. It's going to be an awesome play, hope you can all watch it!!"

The crowd had begun to disperse; The Org members began doing a triumphant jig at the front of the stage while chanting what Patrice thought was their organization's song; the rest of the Phi Delta Phi members emerged from the tent, now unneeded for auctioning and all looking, Patrice thought, profoundly relieved. Patrice was heading up the stairs when Jon caught up with her.

"Patrice, are you going back to Alta?"

"Yes, Jon. You?"

"Back to the apartment," he said. "May I walk with you?"

"Sure, I guess," said Patrice, feeling awkward. She wasn't close friends with Jon and didn't relish the thought of making stilted small talk with him as they walked home; still, it seemed rude to decline. They passed the Greek pavilion and the bridge by the Co-Op in silence. As they walked in the darkened street behind the Humanities building, however, Jon seemed to pluck up the courage to talk.

"How have you been, Patrice?"

"Er, I'm okay…you know, the usual, acads, football, keeping afloat," she ventured. "Um. You?"

"Oh, doing well, doing well."

"Great."

Now they were at the Management classrooms and Patrice silently prayed their walk would speed up so she could finally get back to her books.

Jon cleared his throat. "Paul is doing fine, too."

"That's—that's nice to know," she said, wondering where he was going with this.

"He wanted to come out tonight but, ah, he had to study. Fi—"

"—Finals coming up, yeah—"

"Yes, and too bad because he'd been saying he wanted to see people other than the ones in the Math building. You know, all the usual suspects. He misses the crowd at Humanities. He misses ENG 5 too." Jon infused his tone with a meaning that Patrice couldn't—or was determined not to—catch.

"Yeah, well, it was a shame he had to drop it. Nadia said he had a pretty good paper."

"Yeah, a shame…" Jon trailed off. Now they crossed the street to Raymundo Gate and Patrice willed with all her heart that this odd conversation would end.

"Patrice, OK, I'm going to tell you something, but you have to promise me you will not tell anyone about it," he said suddenly. "Do you swear?"

"Jon, I don't—"

"Do you swear?"

"Fine, I swear. What's this about?"

"That whole thing with The Org, the auction? That wasn't my idea at all. I had nothing to do with it. Well, initially."

"Huh?" Patrice stopped in front of a corner barbecue grill where an old lady tended coals with a woven fan. "Hold a sec, Jon, let me just grab a bite, I'm starving." She paid for a pork skewer and he followed her lead. Munching on the charred, sweet, smoky meat, she said, "Continue."

Jon swallowed. "As I was saying, it wasn't my idea at all. It was Paul's."

"Paul's?" She hastily closed her mouth to keep a piece of pork from falling out. To say she was astonished was an understatement. She could not connect the cheeky, raucous evening she had just witnessed with the reserved, arrogant man she knew.

"He'd seen Bit-Bit's plea shared all over Facebook. I don't know, Patrice, he must've gotten sick of reading it—I mean, it's been shared over fifty times—so one night he talked to me and Migs and said we should volunteer to help them out."

"With a *slave auction*?!"

"No—no," Jon hastily added. "Not at first. The plan was to have the brods have a day of service; as in, do chores like paint your *tambayan* or clean an org house or wash cars for a small fee. We were pretty cool with that. And then, well— we went to talk with Bit-Bit and Claude and The Org's officers and they started throwing out all these ideas and one thing led to another and well, there you go, the 'day of service' became a slave auction."

"Why'd you guys still do it?" asked Patrice.

"Bit-Bit and Claude can be, well, *persuasive.* And...Paul convinced us to go through with it. It was for a good cause, he said. It wouldn't look good for the frat if we backed out, he said. It'd be fun, he said. And...well, he promised that we could have our sem-ender at his family's resort for free if we did."

"Man, Jon, you sound just like the meme: 'Go to the auction, he said. It'll be fun, he said...'"

Jon had to snicker.

"I have to say, though, now you don't sound quite so cool knowing that Paul practically bribed you into doing it," she teased. "I wonder what his ulterior motive could be."

Jon turned serious. "No ulterior motives, no hidden agendas, Patrice. He really, genuinely wanted to help out." She concentrated on the last bit of pork clinging to the barbecue stick. "But just between you and me, and I know he'll kill me if he knew I'm saying this, *I* suspected a small, personal motive. It's just that...He's a really nice guy, Patrice. I don't know what's going on, but I'm not stupid. I know you guys fought. But, yeah, like I said, he's a really good guy. It takes a while to get to know him, but when you do—"

"Did he put you up to this?" she interrupted.

"No, I swear," he held his hand up. "Believe me, Patrice, if he knew I was talking to you about this now he'd freak out. He hates having his business discussed and this is way beyond what he'd tolerate."

"So why are you telling me this?" she demanded.

He looked lost and uncomfortable. "I don't really know. Maybe it's because I can't stand getting all the credit for something I didn't do. I mean, he specifically said that it was a Phi Delta Phi matter and it wouldn't be right for him to be directly involved, and logically I represent the frat as president and all. But still. I just can't stand getting any praise for it. Maybe if at least *you* knew the truth—well, that would kind of ease my conscience a bit. That's why I'm telling you all about this. Can you accept that?"

Patrice opened her mouth to argue and then closed it a moment later, settling for a nod in agreement. "I guess I can, Jon," she sighed. "And anyhow, it doesn't change the fact that all of you did a really cool thing for The Org. I'm glad you got talked into it." The skewers finished and discarded, they resumed their walk home.

"Thanks," he laughed, and then suddenly stopped. Exiting from the convenience store a block from Alta and U.S.A., loaded with instant ramen, hot chocolate sachets and a huge bag of chips, was the topic of conversation. Paul stopped dead in his tracks and almost gaped as Jon and Patrice approached. Jon, Patrice noticed with concern, looked as shifty and guilty as a thief stuck in a window. "Get it together, Jon," she whispered.

Paul recovered quickly. "Jon. Patrice."

"Paul," she answered, feeling a little more warmly towards him than she had before. She looked over his stash. "Fueling?"

He shifted from side to side. "Yes. Loads of exams to study for. I'm a bit of a snacker when I'm, er, stressed." He looked between the two of them and cleared his throat. "On your way home? Mind if I join you?"

"Sure," Jon answered.

"So," Paul addressed Jon as they walked. "How was the auction?"

"Went well," he said, and Patrice wanted to kick him for the supremely embarrassed look on his face, which she was sure Paul had noticed—he studied his housemate's face with a suspicious look in his eyes. "They made their target early so the rest of the brods didn't have to get up."

"That's good then," said Paul. "Who was the last?"

"Migs."

"Ah." Now it was Paul's turn to look guilty. What was *with* these two? "Where you there, Patrice?" he asked.

"Yes. It was fun," she said, adding: "Gia was there too."

"I hope she had a good time." His tone dripped with meaning.

"I'm sure she did," she replied, thankful as the outline Alta loomed in front of them. "Well, here I am. Thanks for, uh, walking me home Jon. Paul," she nodded.

"Can I take you to the gate?" he said, leaving Jon after a whispered discussion.

"OK."

Apparently the walk of awkwardness was not over yet.

"I, uh—" Paul began. "I hope you're doing well?"

"Fine enough, thanks."

They stopped at Alta's gate, in front of the patio where they had last, disastrously, spoken. Patrice stood there, waiting as Paul seemed to struggle to say something. In his house clothes—a frayed pair of basketball shorts, slippers and a well-worn and comfy-looking T-shirt—and arms loaded with snackables, he looked more approachable, more human somehow.

Maybe Jon's shared little secret did its trick on her, after all.

"Well," he blurted out. "Good luck with your exams."

"Thanks."

"And your game on Saturday. Hope you win," he stammered.

"I hope so too," she said, pushing the creaky, wrought-iron door open. "Bye Paul."

"Bye, Patrice," he said, smiling as he turned home—this couldn't be the first time she had ever seen him *smile*, could it?

Completing her analysis of *A Modest Proposal* helped her get her mind off the evening's oddness, but Patrice's surprises weren't over yet. At eleven, way past her usual bedtime, Gia entered their room, a carnation in one hand and a giant grin on her face. She tried to cross to her bed as nonchalantly as possible, but Patrice couldn't let her get away with that.

"And where have you been?!" she teased, tossing a pillow at her roommate.

Gia tried to suppress another wide smile but failed. Sinking to her bed, she swooned, "Oh, Patits!"

She lay like that for a few minutes, looking utterly happy. "I can't—I don't—I'm just—*oh*! How can I even say what I feel?"

Patrice laughed. "I think I might have an idea. So, come on, out with it! Tell me everything."

Gia propped herself up on her elbows. "He took me to dinner—nothing over the top, it was all very casual and comfy. We ate, had a little coffee, talked; he gave me this—" she brought the carnation to her face. "It was perfect," she inhaled deeply.

Patrice joined her on the bed. "…And?" she giggled. "What else? Did he explain anything? Did he apologize? Did he…*woo* you?"

Gia laughed. "*Woo* is such an old-fashioned word, Patits…but you know what? I think that's *exactly* what he did." She started drifting off in her own little world again.

"Earth to G, Earth to G, Patrice wants the *chika* now, do you read me?"

Gia laughed again. "Fine, Patits, I copy you. Yes, we talked. He said…he said that he was sorry for behaving like such an ass at that party. He said it was just that—that he felt like I didn't like him at all."

Patrice bit her tongue to keep from blurting out what she knew.

"And at first that put me off but then I realized…well, I'm kind of to blame for that, wasn't I, Patits? Here I was completely ignoring him and avoiding him because I was so embarrassed about what happened at his place the night Marga invited me over—I mean, what was he *supposed* to think?"

"But what made him finally change his mind?"

"He said that he missed me, that he thought we had a nice thing going, and that it was a shame that it was cut off so soon, just when he thought it was going to bloom. And that he—" and here she shut her eyes and smiled "—and that he hadn't tried hard enough. That he had given up too easily. He said he realized this when he was reading stuff online and came across this quote by Bob Marley. He said he felt punched in the stomach when he saw it:

"'If she's amazing, she won't be easy. If she's easy, she won't be amazing. If she's worth it, you won't give up. If you give up, you're not worthy.'"

Patrice made a low, whistling sound. "Boy's got game."

Gia tossed the pillow back at her. "Crazy! Anyway…once the frat was committed to the human auction, he decided it was time for one big move—a 'one time big time' gesture where he would know, once and for all, if I really liked him or not. So he decided to be part of the auction."

"That's nuts! What if you didn't show up? What if you didn't claim him?" she shook her head. "It was a pretty big gamble for him to take."

"I know, Patits. And that explains a bunch of things...like why Bit-Bit and Claude and the rest of The Org have been bugging me on Facebook and in classes about how I *had* to be at the auction, etcetera."

"They were in on it?"

"Pretty much," she said.

"But I have to say, his big move paid off," said Patrice.

"Oh, you have no idea," said Gia, blushing again. She sat up and clasped Patrice's hands. "Patits, he asked me, formally, to be his girlfriend—"

Patrice pulled her hands free and stuffed a pillow against her face to keep her shrieking from being heard.

"—and Patits, I said yes!"

"OHMYGODOHMYGODOHMYGOD," Patrice cried breathlessly, getting up and pulling her friend into a big hug. "I'm so happy for you, G! So happy!"

"Thank you, thank you!" said Gia, squeezing Patrice tightly. "I'm so happy too!"

They sank to the bed and laughed, both giddy and excited. "Oh Patits...if only you could be this happy —"

"Now G, don't start. This is your moment, remember?"

"*My* moment?"

"Yes, *your* moment. Enjoy it, savor it! No need to worry about your troll roommate."

Gia gently pulled Patrice's ponytail. "You're *hardly* trollish, Patits." Her expression suddenly turned serious. "But honestly. I feel like a bottle of soda that's been shaken up so much; like I want to explode and there's just no way to let it out. I've never had this feeling before...and I wish with all my heart that there could be a guy who could make you feel as I do now. "

Patrice felt something like a small stab in her heart. Gia did look exquisitely happy, joyful even; her cheeks were bright with emotion and there was a smile on her face that seemed to reach all the way into her soul. What would she give to have a smile like that on *her* own face?

She prodded at the stab, that twinge of heartache…it wasn't envy that she felt now but something a little mournful; a little like loss. Covering the sudden sadness in her thoughts with a wry expression, she joked, "Well, we can't all have your luck, Gia Delgado. Besides, maybe there's some crashing bore from Agri or, I dunno, Forestry lurking in the campus that I've yet to meet. He'll bore me to tears; I'll drive him nuts—it'll be just what I wanted!"

"Crazy," Gia said again. "But enough about me, please! Oh, but I can't sleep; I'm too excited. Tell me something, anything—did you talk with any of The Org after the auction? Pick up any gossip? Share, Patits?"

"Nah, didn't get a chance to say hi to Bit-Bit—all The Org looked like they were gearing up to party hearty, and you know how hard that crowd goes…not that you would've noticed," she winked, racking her head for something to distract the amped-up Gia and finally hitting on a topic. "But wait! Yes, now that you mentioned it, I *have* got some juicy gossip I can share with you." And she proceeded to fill Gia in on her earlier conversation with Jon.

"But G, you have to swear not to tell anyone," Patrice finished.

"I—I swear, Patrice," Gia's eyes were round as saucers. She got up and paced the room. "But still! I'm shocked. Why on earth would Paul get involved with The Org? I mean, yes, Jon said he wanted to help out. But why them, and why now?"

"I know right? It's the strangest thing. I swear, G, I've never met a guy as hard to figure out as Paul Dalmacio."

Gia turned to her with a crafty, suspicious, most un-Gia-ish look.

"What?" said Patrice.

"Nothing," said Gia with forced innocence. She paced again then suddenly sat beside Patrice. "Look, OK, hear me out Patits: I know you say you hate him and all but I've always suspected he likes you, and you haven't been seeing each other, right, so what if all this is a play to get your attention?"

"What? Are you crazy?" said Patrice. "Is this what happens when you're in love, G? You start seeing love-schemes even when they're not there?"

"I know it sounds far-fetched but you have to admit, it's really strange, right?" Gia said excitedly. "Do you really buy the selfless act Jon is selling? And why all the secrecy?"

"Yes, but—" Even as she thought of all the ways to rebut Gia's suggestion she couldn't deny her heart was beating madly. What if it were true? Far-fetched as it was, what if Paul really did it for her? Did he still like her? Her pulse raced as she considered it. Now that she knew a bit more about him than before, she found that she didn't find his attention as repulsive as she first did. But when she gave in to her other thoughts, her heartbeat slowed, and the sadness she'd tried to hide returned. After she behaved so badly towards him, it seemed impossible for him to still like her.

Besides: "G, let's be reasonable here. If he just wanted to catch my attention there are other, easier ways of doing it. Involving his friend's frat…doesn't that sound like so much effort for so little return?"

"'If she's worth it, you won't give up. If you give up, you're not worthy,'" quoted Gia.

"Whatever, rasta girl," she rolled her eyes.

"But you have to admit, the auction did get your attention," pressed Gia.

"It did," she admitted.

"And anyway, if I'm wrong, and this is all a truly selfless act, then maybe you misjudged him after all," finished Gia.

"It seems that I have," said Patrice, feeling that stab in her heart deepen once again.

Chapter 11

Heartache notwithstanding, Patrice's last ten days of classes was finally starting to look up. Gia and Migs were always hanging out at the dorm, and where Deenie and Lars made everyone feel awkward and uncomfortable, these two seemed to radiate a sweetness that everyone—even the stoic Miss Alya—seemed to absorb and reflect in a big bubble of cute.

Patrice especially liked hanging out with them: Migs was smart and easy and able to talk about anything under the sun; Gia laughed more often and seemed more playful when he was around. The self-mastery that Patrice hadn't realized was in place all these years slowly gave way to a girl who was genuinely relaxed and in-the-moment. And even if their patio huddles were constantly interrupted by Mrs. Timbol, who for some reason seemed to believe that Migs and Gia was all *her* doing, Patrice still felt happy and secure with her best friend and her best friend's boyfriend. It was almost like being part of a family, a real, nuclear one, with brothers and sisters; not the lonely existence at home with her aunt.

But there was, still, a fly in the ointment. Deenie was increasingly absent from the dorm, and with Pam and Aleli unexpectedly buckling down to finals week, studying up a storm on the mezzanine, her standard "Pam and Aleli chaperone me" excuse went up in flames. Gia cornered a suddenly shifty Isay in the kitchen, who broke down and confessed that Deenie had dropped six of her 18 units and was on the verge of failing another subject. Worried, Gia told Miss Alya and Mrs. Timbol, who then promptly placed the girl on "lockdown," giving her a strict curfew and assigning the freshmen dormers Isay and Rebecca to keep tabs on her classes. "We were entrusted by her mother!" said Mrs. Timbol, who liked to explode with the story at random times of the day. "We will not be accused of being irresponsible house mothers!"

Patrice did her best to keep well away from the unfolding drama, and Saturday's semi-finals match against Alejo College seemed to be the best antidote. In a repeat of the game against Blessed Mother, the University was on fire: more a football machine than a team of eleven athletic girls, they demolished their opponents, coming back from a one-goal deficit in the first half to win the match with a score of 4-1. They were now on a collision course with their arch-rivals St. Clements on the tournament finals, to be held the weekend after classes officially ended.

The team was in high spirits as they pulled up in front of the Student Union cafeteria. The coach promised them all lunch; they'd texted and posted about the match, and before they knew it there were twenty or so people milling by the cafeteria entrance breaking into applause as they disembarked, and Kitty was near tears as she announced that their friends came together for a "flash victory party."

Gia, Aleli, Pam and even Deenie were among the well-wishers. Someone thrust a red plastic cup in Patrice's hand: pomelo juice with that familiar, plastic-y aftertaste of cheap gin. She wheeled around to see Aleli surrounded by the cups and manning what looked like Alta's old water jug just by the common smoking area. Soon everyone was celebrating in a long communal table with baked macaroni and *pancit*; people kept on slipping into the 7-11 next door and emerging with giant bags of Lala Fish Crackers and Clover chips for everyone to share; and Patrice was laughing and talking so much she could almost forget the ache in her muscles and the old anxiety in her heart.

"Refill," Aleli whispered in her ear, and off they went to clandestinely tip a fresh bottle of gin and a sachet of juice into the jug. Patrice exchanged greetings with acquaintances on smoking break while Aleli told the line that followed them to be patient, refreshments were on their way.

Gia was all smiles as she walked to the Phi Delta Phi *tambayan*, where Migs and his brods were hanging out. As the oldest and most prestigious fraternity in the University, they—and their sister sorority, Phi Gamma Chi—were accorded the informal honor of having their *tambayan* by the special sunken common areas in the Student Union building. Patrice could make out Marga Mañalac and her sisses watching them.

She pushed the uneasiness away when Gia came back, trailed by Migs, Jon Lee…and Paul.

"Congrats, guys!" Migs and Jon said, mingling with everyone on the gin pomelo line (the party, in the weird mob sentience parties often display, had moved from the cafeteria to the smoker's area).

But Patrice had eyes only for Paul. Her heart started to beat a little quicker as he stood beside her and said:

"Congratulations. Well played."

"Thanks," she said. "Did you just get here? Didn't see you at the *tambayan*."

"Oh, I was out back, by the creek. I'm not really comfortable hanging out with the whole frat—I'm not a brod, after all."

Patrice remembered Lars' accusation about Paul's connections with the fraternity and blushed.

"Actually, I just dropped by to get my notes from Migs. Still need to study."

"Oh."

"Lucky I ran into you," he said.

Suddenly she felt unable to meet his eye. The trouble was that when she did, she saw things there that made her feel…other things. Things like tenderness. And regard. And self-consciousness. And a whole lot of something that felt like affection.

"Well, I—"

"Why don't you join us?" she said at the same time as him. "Come on. It's a Saturday. You can keep from the books for a few hours, right?"

Was that *another* rare Paul Dalmacio smile?

"I guess I could."

Cups of spiked juice in hand, they mixed with the team and their friends, Patrice joking and talking, Paul attempting a comment every now and then but never leaving her side even when the comments fell flat. Patrice caught a meaningful glance from Gia, which she pretended not to notice, and Deenie couldn't resist letting loose with a loud and attention-getting: "Look who's *friends* now!" Patrice blushed when people turned and started teasing, but Paul placed his hand on the small of her back to reassure her.

That was what probably did it.

Marga Mañalac and a couple of her sorority friends detached from their table and approached.

"Marga!" Jon, of course, took up host duties and welcomed her to the group.

"Hey," she said acidly. She accepted a cup from Aleli and exchanged small talk with some people. Patrice watched her circle them, feeling like she belonged to a school of tuna.

Gia took one look at Marga and then pulled Migs into the cafeteria with her.

"Paul," said Marga, approaching now, scenting blood on the water. "Haven't seen you in a while."

"Busy. You?"

"Same old same old," she grinned her Great White smile at Patrice.

"Marga."

"I heard you won, eh?"

"It's why we're here."

"Nice. That's real talent. I guess the whole 'practice makes perfect' thing is overrated."

Patrice had to frown at that. "Uh…what?"

"Oh, unless you didn't play, of course? Because then it'll just be a case of keeping the out-of-practice ones on the bench, yes?"

"What the hell are you talking about?"

Marga affected an innocent 'what are *you* talking about' counter-stare. "*You* know. How you haven't been practicing and stuff?"

Patrice shook her head. "I have no idea where you heard that, because if you ask anyone in the team—anyone here right now—they'll tell you I'm *always* there." It was a simple thing to accuse someone of slacking off, but Patrice took it extra personal. Anyone knew that next to school, football was her top priority. Saying she took it for granted was like branding her a fake.

"Oh, but that's not what *I* heard," trilled Marga.

"What's this about, Marga?" asked Paul.

"I don't supposed *you* know anything about it, Paul, as it concerns your most favorite person in the world, but my dear Patrice, you should really check what your friend Lars is saying about you."

She couldn't trust herself to speak, but Marga wouldn't stop.

"He talks about it all over U.S.A. Gosh, even Mang Boy at the convenience store knows that you two are pretty hot and heavy. He said you made your football practices an excuse and you were actually out with him the whole time. That you guys even role play in your uniform."

Patrice felt Paul freeze beside her. She didn't know what to say—the outright absurdity of it blindsided her—and she was just thinking of what to reply when she heard a gasp behind her.

"So it's true," said Deenie. She was so still , so motionless; only the welling tears in her eyes moved.

"Deenie—"

"I heard the rumors, Patrice; Lars tried to keep them from me but I heard. I didn't believe them because my God, how? But everyone knows it, so it must be true!"

Irritation flared in Patrice's belly like a flame. "Don't be dumb, Deenie; can you actually hear what you're saying? And Marga—"

The poison spread, the task done, all that Patrice could catch of Marga was a sly smirk and a toss of her perfectly groomed hair as she walked out the building.

"Don't call me dumb, Patrice!" Deenie yelled and now people stopped talking and started watching them. Gia and Migs noticed the commotion and hurried back. "He said he wasn't really into you. He said you came on to him. At the mid-term party. I knew you were there, Patrice, you can't lie!"

Aleli came to pull Deenie away. "You have it all wrong, Deenie, I was there too—"

But Deenie wasn't listening. "Explain *that*, Patrice!"

"Deenie, I swear—"

"Didn't you like him? We all knew it; you'd practically throw yourself at him at Alta."

Patrice felt Paul ever so slightly step away from her side.

"Deenie, come on," said Pam.

"Why are you all taking *her* side?" Deenie was shaking now. "Is it because I'm just a lowly little freshman? You all think that I'm wrong about this and Patrice is not; that Lars somehow duped me? You all *suck*!"

"Wait—" Patrice took Deenie's hand.

"Oh spare me the holier-than-thou act, Patrice!" Deenie practically spit at her face. "We all know where it's been!" Pushing past her, she ran out the Student Union building.

It took a while for Patrice to realize that she, too, was shaking. Her hands were as cold as ice, yet her face burned. She looked at the faces watching her: some looked sympathetic, some looked amused, still others had that bright-eyed look people had before they texted their friends *You wouldn't guess what happened today*. Finally she looked at Paul. Wasn't it just a few minutes earlier when she thought she could read so much in his eyes—tenderness, affection, regard? Why couldn't she see anything there now?

"I think I'm tired. I'm going back to the dorm now." She whispered this, but knew everyone heard it.

Chapter 12

"I have to tell Tita Luz," said Gia.

Gia, Aleli and Pam were sitting in Patrice's room, and all they could talk about was Deenie.

And how Deenie was missing.

It had only been for a few hours, but they were getting worried. Deenie did not return any of their messages, nor did she come home that night, so when twelve a.m. came and went, Aleli and Pam got up to waylay Lars at his apartment.

But Lars wasn't there either.

Now the girls spent the rest of the morning contacting their music club brods and sisses, asking if they heard anything from Lars or Deenie, while Gia monitored the laptop to see if either of them would post something—a check-in, a tweet, a cryptic picture; anything that would clue them in as to where Deenie could be.

Meanwhile, the dorm mothers were crazed with worry. Patrice watched them in the patio, from the window by her bed.

She could hear Mrs. Timbol: "My goodness, never in all my years have I come across such a bad dormer, oh Koko, can you believe it? Boy-crazy, irresponsible, thoughtless… Oh!" cried Mrs. Timbol.

She could see Isay, by Mrs. Timbol's side, working a woven fan into a blur. On the other was a lost-looking Rebecca Jobilo, who tried to get Mrs. Timbol to drink from a glass of water that she kept on waving away.

"It's that—that *boy*! He is a bad influence! Oh girls, did I not tell you *never* to go to U.S.A.? A den of sin!" She dissolved into wordless wails.

"Isay, Rebecca, please help me bring Mrs. Timbol inside," said Miss Alya, and the two freshmen each took an arm and helped Mrs. Timbol up. "*Ate*, I don't think being in the patio is good for you. The heat."

They could hear Mrs. Timbol still wailing as they proceeded inside. A door slammed shut downstairs, cutting off her monologue.

"It's only eight, Gia, we could find them by then," said Pam, but her tone was losing its hopefulness.

"Guys, no," Gia shook her head. "I should've called Tita Luz last night." The phone in her hand suddenly began to buzz. She frowned as she stared for several seconds at the screen, and then hurried outside to take the call.

Patrice was on her bed, too numb and dazed to be of use to anyone. She worried about Deenie too, but most of all she was in shock. Angry and shocked.

After leaving Student Union, she had been ready to march straight to Lars' apartment and tear him a new one, but Gia, Pam and Aleli convinced her not to. What if Deenie was there, they said to her, and the two of them got into a fight? She could almost see Lars—cherubic, charming, two-faced Lars—smugly watching them go at it. He would probably tell all his friends about how two chicks went and fought over him, wasn't that cool, dudes? Would she really want to give him *that* satisfaction, Gia had asked.

But then what should she do? Stay here and cower and just hope the last few days of school would end already? Avoid Raymundo Street in the hopes of bypassing him and his friends, just as Gia once did with Migs? She felt impotent and confused and angry. Most of all, she felt humiliated.

And then there was Paul. As her thoughts chased each other more often than not they stopped to dwell on the look on his face before she said goodbye. *Did* he believe Marga? Or the source, Lars? Patrice couldn't say for sure. Her past behavior certainly supported Lars' lies. She flashed back to the night of the mid-term party; how he had suddenly appeared and put his arms around her, just as if they were together, and how Paul abruptly shut up and left them. It filled her with embarrassment.

So maybe Paul was back in U.S.A. now, pissed at her, thinking that she and Lars had been, as Marga put it, "hot and heavy." But so what? Why was the thought making her so upset? Yes, it was a bald-faced lie, and that pissed her off tremendously; but it was more than that. As she thought about it, the more she realized that what she couldn't bear was the thought of Paul Dalmacio, BS Applied Math, who had once told her he had feelings for her and who was capable of acts of kindness she had never expected, was out there somewhere thinking badly of her.

Gia re-entered the room, staring at her phone like it would explode any minute. Aleli glanced from her laptop-monitoring duties. "Well? Was that Tita Luz?"

"No," said Gia, still staring intently at the phone. "But I think Deenie's on her way back."

Pam and Aleli exploded into cheers while Gia excused herself to tell Mrs. Timbol and Miss Alya. A few minutes later, Patrice heard a car pull in front of the dorm.

It was silver Toyota. That looked a lot like Paul's.

Patrice sat up, her heart hammering wildly. The driver's door opened and Paul emerged—it *was* his! But before she could wonder what he was doing here, the passenger door opened...and out stepped Deenie.

"Huh?" Patrice couldn't help but say. Pam and Aleli were too busy doing the dance of joy to hear her. She watched from the window as Paul and Deenie talked, too soft to hear. But it was clear from Deenie's body language—the crossed arms, the averted head—that she didn't like what she was hearing.

Paul rang the bell and now Patrice could see Gia run outside, take Deenie's hand, and *hug* Paul?

"Huh?" she said again, feeling like the slowest kid in remedial class.

"She's back!" Gia called as they entered the dorm. Pam and Aleli shot out the door as a mad scramble of footsteps rushed out the other dorm rooms and down the stairs.

Patrice got up and followed them. Whatever was going on, Gia had a lot of explaining to do.

Chapter 13

The last five days of class passed by in a blur of red-lined blue books, end-of-semester meetings with professors, class card returns and some truly torturous football practices. It was all so busy and whirlwind that Patrice had even forgotten to dwell on the strange developments at Alta, its inhabitants, and those at the neighboring apartment complex U.S.A.

Well, almost.

She still couldn't stop to think over the strangeness of the Deenie Situation, which was what everyone in Alta was now calling the episode. Deenie had returned, all sad-eyed and chastised and weird, but she couldn't seem to face any of her dormmates and instead went straight to Miss Alya's room, where they talked in private. The girls were left to speculate on their own theories until Mrs. Timbol came out, looking a lot more cross and annoyed than usual, and ordered them all to return to their rooms. A few minutes after that, a black SUV pulled up at Alta's gates. It was Deenie's mom.

It had seemed that Miss Alya called her a few hours after Deenie went missing; and when her daughter hadn't returned the next day she drove up to the University in a panic. It was a small comfort that Deenie *was* there when she arrived, but there was still a tremendous screaming match with Mrs. Timbol about how they were irresponsible and did not take care of her daughter, etc. It ended with Deenie running upstairs…and tearfully packing all her belongings.

Remembering it made her feel awful and sorry for Deenie all over again. With just a week of school left, Deenie's mom decided that the University was too much for her daughter and pulled her out, determined, she said, to put her somewhere else. Preferably run by nuns, where there were no boys or sororities or raging parties that would distract her from her studying. Deenie strongly felt the loss and sobbed as she hugged Gia goodbye. She even whispered a small "sorry" to Patrice before she left.

"You see, not everyone is cut out for the University and all its freedoms," was all that Miss Alya had to say about *that*.

As for what drove Deenie back to the dorm, all the girls pestered Gia, who had brought her in the door and *should* have been the most in-the-know; but Gia said she was as lost as they were. Patrice confronted her about it one night, owning that she had seen Paul drop Deenie off, but all Gia would say was that Paul and Lars had a common acquaintance who lived by the Faculty Co-Op on the upper campus, and he had traced Lars and Deenie there. As to what he said to make Deenie leave Lars, Gia didn't know: in the relief of having Deenie back she didn't think it right—or relevant—to ask.

Now her thoughts walked that same well-trod path again. She tried stopping herself from doing so, but she still missed Paul. Every time she left the dorm to go to class or practice or a meeting she wished she would run into him, but like so many things she fervently wished for, it did not come true. Disappointed, she tried to accept the fact that the semester would end without seeing him, without her finding out what he had to do with the Deenie Situation, and without them making up.

"Patrice, if I have to tell you one last time to get it together I'm going to lose it," the coach said. Patrice was supposed to be stretching but had drifted off, lunged in a runner's stretch that should have ended minutes ago.

"Come on, girl, don't be nervous. We can take them on!" said Catch, trying to be chipper but betraying her own nerves with the quake in her voice.

Patrice shook her head and apologized; now was not the time to let her concentration waver. It was the regional football championships, against their old rivals St. Clement's, to be played at the University's own football field by the old Carillon bell tower. Now, more than ever, she needed to focus and get her head in the game.

The coach checked his watch and signaled the team together.

"OK, girls. Here we are. The big one." His eyes were shining and he grimaced. "It's been a long journey. A crazy

semester." (*You don't know the half of it*, thought Patrice.)
"And now look at us. Almost, but not quite at, the end of our
journey. Girls, I just want to say that I am so proud of you. A
coach could not ask for a better team." He was choked with
emotion. "I know there is so much in you, and I know we
can do more than we ever did before. So when you step on
the field, I want you to take what is yours. Show St.
Clement's and show the University what you've got. Let's do
it!"

With yells like battle cries they echoed his call and ran
out to the field, skipping over its width to warm up.

The St. Clement's girls soon followed, immaculate in
their white uniforms to the University's maroon, warming up
as well. The grandstand's benches hosted sparse groups of
spectators who were still in campus on a Saturday, while the
sloping ground that flanked the field attracted scores of
picnickers and afternoon joggers drawn by the unusual
spectacle of an actual football match. St. Clement's own
ragtag band of supporters claimed the first row of the stands,
waving their school's banner.

The players lined up and the referee talked to them
about a "good, clean game."

Patrice swallowed a lump past her throat as she shook
hands with the St. Clement's squad and took her position on
field. This was it. The big game they all trained for. The cap
to a crazy semester. Her stomach not only hosted butterflies
but grizzly bears and galloping horses; her hands were numb
and ice cold.

The coin was tossed, the forwards met in the center. The
referee put the whistle in his mouth and blew.

The ball moved quick from forward to winger to
midfielder; lightning-quick passes giving way to strong lobs
in the air. It came to Patrice and she battled another
midfielder for the ball, shoving and blocking each other as
they ran, each throwing an arm out to dislodge the other's
momentum. They scrambled but Patrice won the ball. She
dribbled it up field, saw an opening between two
approaching opponents, faked left and then passed it over to
April, who drove it close to the goal and attempted a shot—
which was ill-timed, as it went wide of the net.

"Ball control!" yelled the coach.

"It's OK, just the first attempt," called out Kitty, who patted April on the back before returning to her position. The St. Clement's goalie kicked the ball to the center of the field, where Patrice waited, on her toes, poised to stop it when its trajectory collided with hers.

It was then that it happened. Her eyes were on the ball, hurtling in the air, straight towards her body; she spread her arms and bent backwards, preparing to chest it. But in the next moment something clattered into her side like a bus; she lost her footing and found her legs in the air while her body dropped sideways to the ground. She instinctively threw a leg out to break her fall, only realizing a split second too late that it was a monumentally terrible decision. She landed and felt a searing pain shoot up from her ankle.

All at once a commotion blew up above her. Curled on the grass, her eyes squeezed shut from the pain, she could hear, as if from far away in the dull red cloud of pain, the shrill piercing sound of the referee's whistle and then a confused babble:

"Dirty tackle!"

"Red card, ref!"

"Come on, stop acting!"

"Acting? Are you insane?!"

"No, Catch, calm down!" it was a male voice now, her coach.

There were sounds of scuffling and pushing.

"Patrice, Patrice, are you all right?"

"We have to take her to the infirmary!"

"Don't we have a medic?'

"Who has a car?"

"I'll do it."

Gentle hands cradled her neck. "Patrice," spoke a soft, familiar voice. "Let me take you to the doctor."

Her eyes fluttered open and focused on a longed-for face. "P-Paul?"

"I'm going to lift you up, OK?" he said. He tried to comfort her with a grin but failed; his face was creased with worry.

"N-no, I can stand, really—" said Patrice, sitting up. She had to bend her leg to get her balance—and promptly hissed in pain.

"Oh no, you don't," said Kitty, shoving a handful of ice on Patrice's ankle and getting a catlike yowl from her.

"But the game," Patrice said, feeling tears well up from pain and disappointment.

"Don't worry about it," said the coach.

"We'll win it for you," said Kitty, sticking out her chin. "But this needs to be looked at. Just go, Patrice."

Patrice sobbed now, but Paul had one arm behind her and the other under her knees; he stood and lifted her easily. "Ssshh," he soothed. "Everything's going to be OK." He carried her to his car while one of the team substitutes walking in front of them, still holding the bag of ice on Patrice's ankle. The sub helped Paul with the door and ran back to the field as he gently placed Patrice in the front seat, rushed inside and drove to the Infirmary.

"Are you OK? Are you comfortable?" he babbled as he drove, sweat beading in his forehead. "Do I need to adjust the seat? Are you thirsty? Did your teammate leave the ice? We're near now, I'm driving up, don't worry, we'll see the doc soon."

The pain was still present but somehow less intense, and Patrice could now open her eyes and see how tightly he gripped the steering wheel and how he bit his lip as they pulled into the Infirmary's parking. Quick as a flash he was out the door and helping her from the car.

"Please Paul, if I lean on you I think I can walk—"

"Don't be stubborn," he said gruffly, lifting her up and carrying her inside the building. There were about five other patients ahead of them in line, so it took a minute or two to attract a nurse in the notoriously inattentive University Health Services. But one soon came over and sat them down, gingerly removing Patrice's cleats and peeling the kneesock away to reveal her brilliantly purple and red ankle, which was also starting to swell. The nurse hurriedly left to tell the doctor.

"It looks awful," moaned Patrice. She tried to wriggle it and had to clutch Paul's arm when a stab of pain shot through it.

"Shhh," Paul soothed again. "It looks like a bad sprain, but nothing worse than that."

"Let's hope," sniffed Patrice. They sat in silence for a few moments, waiting for their turn.

"Listen, I—"

"I wanted to say—"

"No, you go ahead," said Paul.

"I just wanted to say thank you, Paul, for bringing me here," said Patrice, feeling her cheeks warm and unable to look at him. "Lord knows how fast it took you to get to me—"

"I was watching the game," said Paul. "I saw that St. Clement's girl gun for you as soon as the goal kick. When you went down I just had to run and see if you were all right."

Patrice could feel her cheeks burn. "You were watching the game?"

"I watch all your games. Well, except for the first match. I didn't know you too well then." His voice changed, becoming softer. "But the more I got to know you, and hear about you, and the things you loved, the more I wanted to know you, and hear about you, and see you. And I love to see you play."

Patrice chanced a glance at him and saw an expression that took her completely by surprise: his eyes were full of tenderness and affection, even a little hope. She felt overwhelmed and had to turn away.

"Paul," she began tentatively. "Can I ask you something? Two things, actually."

"Whatever you want."

"Did you have anything to do with Deenie returning home last week?" Now it was Paul who looked away as she told him about seeing him drop Deenie off. "I mean you obviously drove her over, but if you did anything else, I also have to thank you for that, because you saved Gia, and Miss Alya and Mrs. Timbol, all of us at Alta, really, from a painful situation."

"I did do something," he confessed. "As soon as I left you I wanted to find her. I wanted to find *Lars*. But I didn't want to get violent—I know you hate that. So Gia and I texted each other, and I knew that Lars would be unable to face Deenie's mother. He's not the kind of guy to stand up for his girl. I would have found him sooner, too—it took me a while to wrangle his number...I kind of had to ask help from Migs and his brods to scare some of Lars' housemates. Anyway," he coughed, "When I got it I gave him a call. I said that I knew where he was, and that Deenie's mother was with me, and a U.P.F. policeman too, and that if he tried to leave, Deenie's mom would have him arrested for kidnapping. It wasn't a particularly honest thing to do, but he fell for it and told me to pick up Deenie from the Co-Op."

"Thank you," said Patrice again. "From me, from Gia, from all of us —"

"If you would thank me, do it for yourself," he said. "Because it was for you. It was all for you."

Patrice was astonished and silent for a few moments.

"What was your second question?" he asked.

"Oh!" said Patrice. "Erm. Why did you help The Org with their auction?" At the look on his face she hastily added, "Please don't be mad at Jon for telling me, I think he just really wanted me to know. It was a real great thing that you did, so kind…"

"The thing with The Org," he smiled ruefully. "It started out because I wanted to prove you wrong. You said I was arrogant and selfish, that I couldn't speak without waiting for a room to applaud. And that bothered me. I was angry with you. But if I was honest with myself it was mostly because I wondered if you were right."

"Oh Paul, don't remind me of the things I said, I was—"

"You were honest," he finished. "Well, when I saw all those fundraising messages, I thought, here's the chance for me to see if I were truly as selfish and credit-seeking as I feared. I would help them out, but they wouldn't know it was me. And it happened! We pulled it off." Then he turned to her and shyly, as though he was afraid she would turn away, held her hand. "But then I just *had* to see you walking down Raymundo that very same night, and I knew you were at the auction too. There was a part of me that wanted blurt out, 'I did it! I'm not as bad as you thought I was,' but the closer you guys came the more that part faded and faded away. All I could think about was how I missed you, and that no matter how hard I tried to forget you or avoid you, I still felt a thrill when I saw you. Standing beside you that night—it was wonderful."

All sorts of confused thoughts scattered through Patrice's head. It was *him*, being so near, holding her hand; she couldn't concentrate so she pulled it back and said, "And Migs?"

"Migs?"

"You've *got* to have something to do with that."

He chuckled. "I *may* have sent him a Tumblr full of Bob Marley quotes, and I *may* have chipped in to pay for his 'ransom.' Bit-Bit set quite a price on him for leaving the auction." He patted her shoulder. "Don't look so worried. Like you said. It was for a good cause."

The pain in her ankle momentarily forgotten, Patrice found the courage to face him.

He immediately caught her hands again and said, "Patrice. I don't know if what I'm going to say will be welcome. But my feelings for you are the same as they were before—stronger, even. If you feel the same way as you did after the mid-terms, just say the word and I'll promise never to bug you ever again.

"Do you…do you still hate me, Patrice?"

A flood of emotions washed over her—joy, wistfulness, hope; a strange elation inflated like a balloon in her core with a sudden realization of just how deeply she cared for him. It was all there, hidden away; she'd tried to bury it with cultivated dislike and busyness and rationalizations but she was never really successful. Warmth spread from her cheeks all the way down to her toes and she smiled, looked him in the eye and shook her head. A wide smile spread on *his* face and he quickly embraced her.

They hugged for some time, feeling comfortable in each other's arms, happy to finally confess to each other the feelings they had held back for so long.

The connection between two people in love can owe so much to chance: a frustrating mix of the right timing of feelings developing at the same pace and reaching the same intensity; waiting for one to make the right move and hoping that other reads it as intended; countermoves; and the final burst of courage to confess and lay oneself open to the acceptance—or rejection—of the other. That they finally came to this point, after a semester of stops and starts and missed connections, gave them both such a sense of relief and happiness that filled their senses and blocked everything out: the dingy infirmary, the shortening line of waiting, snickering, staring patients, the throb of Patrice's ankle.

Paul leaned back to watch all those emotions playing in Patrice's face.

"What are you staring at?" she smiled.

"My girlfriend," he breathed, tilting her chin and bringing his lips to hers.

Epilogue

Yes, the University won the championships. Patrice had to miss the victory party—the doctor specifically asked her to spend the next 48 hours in bed with her leg elevated. Good thing she had the most attentive gentleman nurse, with a conveniently near apartment, to keep her company. It was very cozy.

Glossary

Every school has its own peculiar culture, and since I tried to capture what it felt like to go to UPLB during my time, there may be some terms that don't make as much sense or mean differently to someone outside the school. Here's a quick guide:

Acads: Short for academics, but encompass anything school-related (e.g. classes, projects, papers, etc.)

Apartment: As with any campus, students have a range of on- and off-campus housing options. Apartments, however, are more expensive to rent and are generally unsupervised, so they're the common choice for older students and rich kids.

Azkals: The Philippine National Football Team.

Blockmate: Incoming freshmen are arranged into blocks, usually alphabetically by surname (e.g. all A-I in Block 1, J-S in Block 2, etc.) This block shares most, if not all, class schedules for the first semester.

Brod (and sis): Short for "brother" and "sister." The terms originated from fraternities and sororities and trickled down to all types of organizations.

Class card: Small index cards issued by the University, given to the professor at the start of the semester and returned at the end of classes with grades.

Dyahe: 70's slang for shy or embarrassed.

FAMAS: The Filipino equivalent of the Oscar awards.

Fratman: Technically any guy who is a member of a fraternity, but the term is especially used for the douche-y, spoiling-for-a-fight, annoying ones.

Infirmary (or University Health Services): A fully-functioning, if somewhat understaffed, on-campus hospital.

Ma'am: Informal term for female instructors and professors; males are addressed 'Sir.' Fairly common regardless of school.

Nuno sa punso: Spirits said to resemble little old men that lurk in mounds of earth; they are very unlucky if disturbed.

Orgs: Campus organizations can be academic organizations (such as The Org), varsitarian (membership by geography or province), hobby (scuba-diving, art, mountaineering, music), and fraternities and sororities. Well-known organizations usually get informal nicknames on campus. Since much of the student population of UPLB resides in and around campus and away from home, an organization functions as a surrogate family, and almost everyone belongs to one.

Rumble: Inter-fraternity altercations, usually violent and pointless.

Sister sorority: Most fraternities started out when the University was all-male and added sister-sororities for girls when the school went co-ed. Sister/brother fraternities and sororities basically function as connected, but separate, organizations.

Tambayan: Literally "a place to hang out" in Filipino. Most student organizations need a place on campus where members can congregate. This is usually a *tambayan*: a table with fixed benches. The location of these tables depends on the organizations' connections with the administration; older and more prestigious organizations having better digs.

Author's note

This story was inspired by two favorite things that made a huge impact on my growth as a writer. I discovered my fiction voice at my alma mater, the University of the Philippines at Los Baños (UPLB), the 'University' in *Well Played*. Some years later I read Jane Austen's classic *Pride & Prejudice* and that opened my eyes to the depth and infinite possibilities of the "chick lit" genre. (It's also my go-to read when I'm sad, the literary equivalent of brownie ice cream). In writing this book I wanted something that felt as good to write as to read, something that captured that brownie ice cream feeling, and something that paid homage to what shaped me as a writer.

I'd like to thank the awesome mover-and-shaker Mina V. Esguerra for taking the time to edit this book as well as all for sharing all her indie publishing wisdom. You the bomb! Thank you Tania Arpa for reading the first draft and being a great cheerleader. I'm also grateful to Tina Akot and Badj Mercado for their input on IP and fair use, and my "boyfriend" Karl Michael Domingo for designing the kick-ass cover.

About the Author

Katrina Ramos Atienza, born and bred in Manila,
Philippines, has been writing all her life. She's worked in the
fields of PR and corporate communications while blogging,
freelancing and writing fiction. Four chick lit novels (Pink
Shoes, 2006; The Hagette, 2006; If the Shoe Fits, 2008 and
Shoes Off, 2010) are available in paperback in the
Philippines, while her earlier short fiction works have been
published in Philippine publications and collected in the
Growing Up Filipino II anthology. Well Played is her first
independently published novel. She graduated from the
University of the Philippines at Los Baños and is married
with two kids.

Contact Katrina:
kratienza@aol.com
http://katrinaramosatienza.blogspot.com
twitter.com/iggyatienza
facebook.com/katrinaramosatienza

98823834R00074

Made in the USA
Columbia, SC
03 July 2018